The Class of '63

Pip Wright

ISBN 978-0-9564855-8-8
Published by **Pawprint Publishing**
14, Polstead Close, Stowmarket, Suffolk IP14 2PJ

Other books by Pip Wright

Exploring East Anglia by Bus Pass
Exploring Suffolk by Bus Pass
The Watery Places of Suffolk
News from Essex
Daniel Malden
Lydia
The Chantry, Sproughton
Death Recorded
I Read it in the Local Rag (pub. by Poppyland Publishing)
Thomas Slappe's Booke of Physicke
A Picture History of Margaret Catchpole
Frolic, Fervour & Fornication
Lucky is the Name

Books by Pip & Joy Wright

The Amazing Story of John Heigham Steggall, 'The Suffolk Gipsy'
Newspapers in Suffolk (6 vols)
Grave Reports
Witches in and around Suffolk
Bygone Cotton

See all these at
www.pipwright.com
&
The Diary of a Poor Suffolk Woodman
(with Léonie Robinson, pub. by Poppyland Publishing)
See **www.poppyland.co.uk**

The Class of '63

Pip Wright

The Accounts of Mr. Candler & Bird. Church:wdn.

All saints 1764 Recd. of William Chapman for a years rent, for Halefields seven pounds in full .... £7..0..0

Paid Lords rent for Halefield .. £0..4..6
for pen Ink & paper and writing Accounts .... —15..0
0..19..6

Scholars appointed to go to School & to receive their Cloaths --

Viz.

Thos. Brett.
Saml. Fricker
John Coals
Jery. Sharmen
Henry Roberson
Geo. Buckle
James Nunn
Isaac Pawzey

Contents

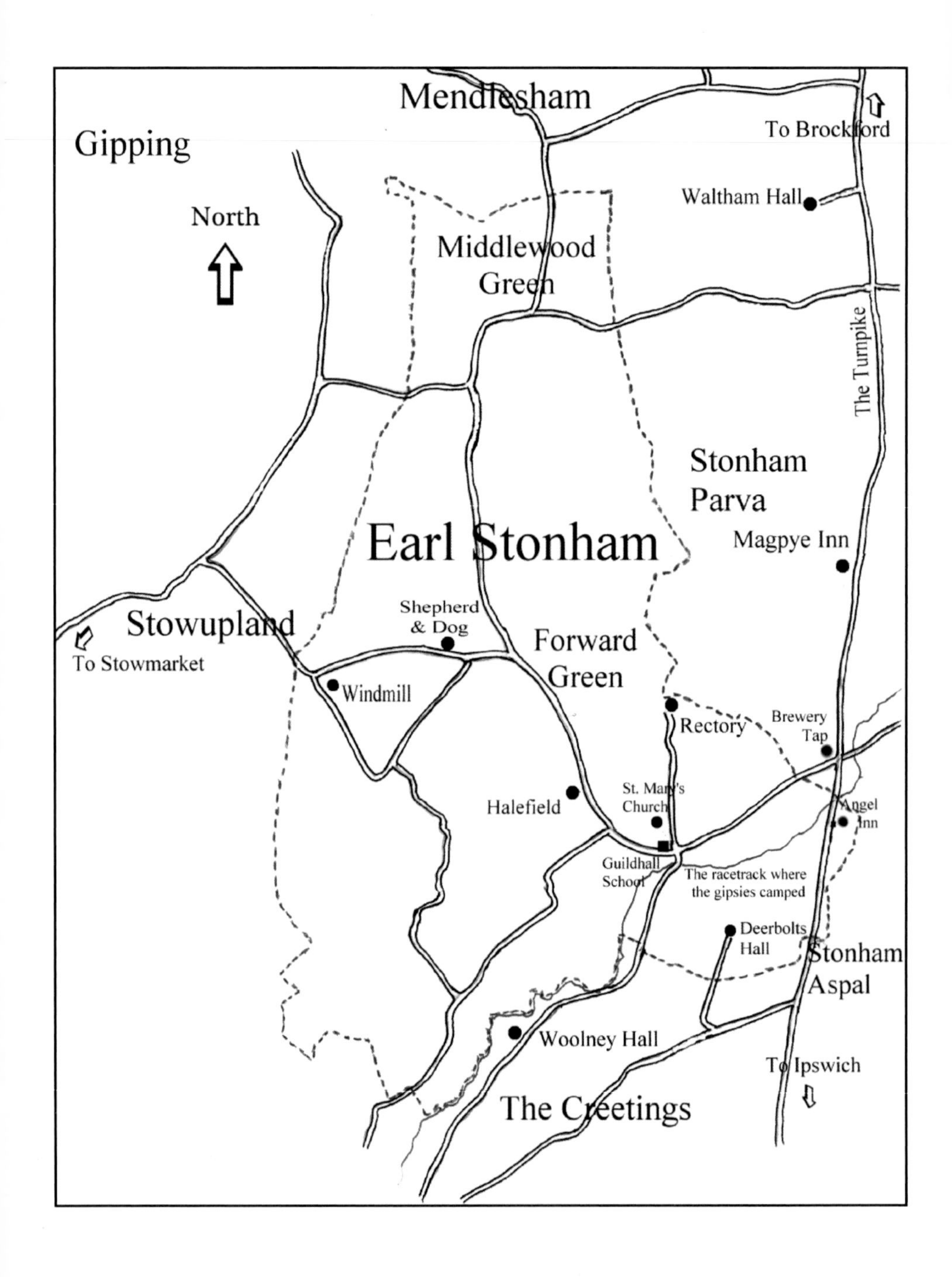
Mendlesham
Gipping
To Brockford
Waltham Hall
North
Middlewood
Green
The Turnpike
Stonham
Parva
Earl Stonham
Magpye Inn
Shepherd
& Dog
Stowupland
To Stowmarket
Forward
Green
Windmill
Rectory
Brewery
Tap
Halefield
St. Mary's
Church
Angel
Inn
Guildhall
School
The racetrack where
the gipsies camped
Deerbolts
Hall
Stonham
Aspal
Woolney Hall
To Ipswich
The Creetings

Spring 1757

"Why are we here?"

There was a long pause whilst Candler Bird considered his reply.

"I suppose you might say because God in His infinite wisdom chose to place us here."

It wasn't an answer and he knew it.

"And why this dreadful place for heaven's sake?" I asked.

This time, his answer was more in tune with my question.

"I thought you as a young man of fashion would appreciate a Coffee House. A place to conduct business! And this is your territory after all."

Possibly - but now I lived twenty miles from Bury; little more than a stroll from the house of the man who was sitting opposite. Why had he dragged me to this squalid establishment when any business we might wish to conduct could have been discussed far more comfortably at home?

I sipped at the black sludge in front of me. It had the taste and consistency of mud. Why my neighbour should have described me as a man of fashion, I have no idea. I have certainly never acquired a taste for coffee, and what was on offer in the Widow's Coffee House was a particularly vile concoction. Added to which, I found the ladies serving it slightly disturbing. I think it was the way they were dressed. Their coverings were not very far removed from those worn by more respectable women in the street outside, but in their case just enough extra flesh was exposed to suggest that their business might extend to a little more than the serving of beverages.

"I have heard say this place is little more than a knocking shop."

Candler Bird's reply this time did little to alleviate my concern.

"Of course it is, and situated just outside the old abbey walls - so, not a lot has changed in the last five hundred years."
He was taking his time, just as he always did. I knew if I waited long enough he would come to the point of our meeting; why we had travelled twenty miles from where we both lived, first by carrier's cart and then by carriage, to be further discommoded before taking the rest of the day to return home.

Something was odd but I couldn't quite put my finger on it to begin with. Then suddenly I realised. I had known Candler Bird for years. He had always spoken with the careless, fractured, musical voice of a Suffolk man of the soil. Now it sounded as if he had been consciously trying to rid himself of the language of his roots. Practically every trace of his Suffolk accent had gone. The timbre of his voice was the same, the chuckle, the gesticulation, the ebb and flow of his intonation were still very much him, but in spite of it all, the voice no longer matched the face.

Outside, it was pandemonium. I had forgotten just how noisy Bury could be on market day: horses snorting and clattering hooves on the cobbles, costers crying their wares, carriages coming and going; the muddle and mayhem of it all.

The Widow's Coffee House was crowded as it usually was. One of a handful of coffee shops in the town, it did a good trade, either in spite of or because of extra benefits to be experienced there. I was quite newly married. I had no desire to sample Mrs. Rooke's girls. Just drinking her coffee was bad enough.

"Do you remember when you were at school," he said, "you and my nephew both lusted after the Master's wife?"

It was true, but we were very young then. The Master had seemed so old and his wife by way of contrast belonged to a different age as far as we could tell. That was how it had seemed all that time ago at Needham Market. During the week, as James Bird and I had too far to travel, we lodged with a couple whose children had all died. They had treated us as their own and I had fond memories of those times - fonder than of the school itself. It had a fine enough reputation, but any sign of a lack of scholarship was the signal for systematic beating. Learning had not come easily to me, and finding a friend in James Bird was possibly the only reason I had lasted the course. He had no such problems. His copy books were immaculate, his accounts faultless. He could converse and read in Latin and knew the Bible, each chapter and verse. He could paint and write verse and do almost anything better than I. But he helped me find my strengths and show the masters that I was worth more than fodder for their brutality.

It started with maps and charts. I had a way of seeing that enabled me to present the world as others couldn't. Not as tidily as James would have done it, but with a precision and an insight that belonged to me alone. So the masters had me show others what I could do, and before I knew it, all those youngsters who had struggled and suffered as I had were learning - from me. Not only map-making; but because learning had not come easily to me, those activities that I had mastered more slowly than others. I had the patience you see. I understood that we didn't all take in the master's words the first time, and before you knew it, I was helping the masters with boys who found it hard to learn. That was when they stopped beating me, and I like to think I saved a number of younger boys from taking a beating too.

"She was a sight fairer than any of these."

"What?" My mind jerked back to the present.

"The Master's wife. I was saying; prettier than Mrs. Rooke's whores."

That was true but it wasn't saying much. Like the establishment they served, they were a pitiful lot.

"We could have met at my club," he continued, "but that would have been a little formal for you and anyway, I've got a certain attachment to this place."

The glass in the windows afforded only a limited view of

the world outside, but I was aware of a good deal of movement on the Angel Hill. It was getting busier. Carriages continued to rumble past. Marketeers shrieked at anyone who turned to face them. Small, bare-footed children, armed with shovels and buckets, struggled to keep the thoroughfares free from what the horses had left behind. Each time the door to the coffee shop was opened, you were assaulted by the noise and the smell. Candler Bird pulled his chair closer to the table. He leaned towards me.

"We could have gone to Mistress Monk's but it's all dealing in there, everyone listening in to everyone's business. Here at least most of the coffee drinkers are otherwise occupied."

"But at home we could have had all the privacy we desired." I still didn't understand.

"I have something I would like you to consider," he said, looking a sight more serious than he had so far.
Then, moving just about as close to me as the table between us would allow, he added, "We have a problem, you see."

"A problem - *we* have a problem or *you* have a problem?"

"How long have you lived in Earl Stonham?" he asked.

Well, that was easy enough - a little under a year. I had been drawn there by my wife Elizabeth. It had all happened so very quickly. On leaving school, I had been sent by my parish to be apprenticed as a wheelwright. An apprentice could find himself a long way from home. It could be a perilous existence; you could be ill-treated and have little chance to complain. You might receive seven years of training in the worst habits from a poor practitioner at his trade. On the other hand, you could be fortunate as I was, up to a point. Six years into my apprenticeship my master, whom I loved and admired, died. I could find no-one to complete my training, so was forced to seek work as a journeyman at wages far below what my skill deserved. I had to take work as and wherever it turned up. Which is how I had come to be in Earl Stonham. My new master's name was Marsh. He had a daughter.

I had known Elizabeth Marsh less than half a year before I married her. Her father was less than enamoured with the idea that I should become his son-in-law. He had hoped for better. Our first months together had been a struggle and I could see no easy way through the years to come. That is probably why I was prepared to accept what Candler Bird was about to offer me.

"You know we finally persuaded old man Ling to resign at the school?" he said.

"I'm sorry, I never really knew him."

"He had been the schoolmaster since 1710 you know." Candler Bird paused before continuing. "He didn't want to go, but he was completely deaf, the boys played him for a fool and it couldn't go on."

"So I understand, but you appointed Jonathan Hart and then out of the blue got rid of him. What was all that about?" I asked.

"A bit too fond of some of the boys, I am afraid. He had to go. Which poses us with a problem. We have a charity school. It goes back to a gentleman by the name of George Reeve around a hundred and fifty years ago. He left land, both in Stonham and in Stowupland, which was to be let to pay a schoolmaster to teach eight boys a year. Also, more land in the parish raised money for the clothes for the boys. The parish supplied the old Guildhall in front of the Church as a schoolroom and home for the Master."

"So what is the problem?" I think I knew by then what was coming next.

"We have been several months without a schoolmaster. We cannot neglect the boys any longer. But the remuneration is only as much as the rent on the charity lands produces and I regret to say it has hardly risen in a hundred years. Experienced school-masters are not exactly beating a path to our door."

"And just how much are we talking about?"

"Eight pounds," he said.

"A year?" Even to one as poorly paid as myself it seemed

derisory. "I suspect your charitable donor, George Reeve, would be appalled were you to appoint what that miserable wage would probably command... some dreadful dame... or worse." The odd thing was that I was actually giving this offer some consideration. "Why do you have to clothe them? That must cost almost as much as their tuition?"

"It does," he answered, "but the details of the Trust require it and besides if we were not to offer the clothing what would attract poor families to send their sons to school when they could be working the land with their fathers."

I wondered what Elizabeth would make of this. She had been intrigued when I had left the house with the day yet to dawn.

"I remember the way James said you used to instruct the boys at Needham. And you were so young then. I feel a confidence in your being the perfect choice. You would of course have free lodging, though the large room would also serve as the schoolroom. And I am sure the parish would agree to supply fuel - shall we say six waggon-loads of wood a year. We can't have you or the boys freezing to death down there."

I knew what he meant. Most of the parish was on the high ground, many of the houses built around ancient greens. But the parish church and a handful of properties were down beside the river where it was known to be damp and cold. The Guildhall was a building that had once been fine enough, but a century or more of neglect had left it in a precarious state. It was hard to see how even my wife Elizabeth could turn it into a home. It was not comfortable in any sense of the word. Down there was a world of mists and osier beds and regular flooding. Even the Rectory was away over the hill.

"Do I have to decide straight away?"

"No, but the boys have been long enough without their education. Give it your thought, but I would appreciate knowing your answer... you know, quite soon."

I think I already knew what my answer was going to be, but I did have to explain to Elizabeth that she would no longer be living with a man whose hands were permanently black and scarred. And I suppose Candler Bird also knew as my next question was, "What should I teach them?"

If he was prompted to assume my decision was made, he didn't show it.

"They come to the school for two, perhaps three years. In that time, it seems reasonable that they should learn to read the Bible, write their name, keep accounts and anything else the master should think appropriate... even map making."

"I am not expected to teach Latin or Greek?"

"I should say not, but all these things are battles you will have to fight for yourself *if...*" and here he paused "*...if* you are prepared to take up my offer. You see, there are men in the village, Mr. Driver for example, who are properly educated - King Edward's School at Bury or better - to these people a classical education is the only education. As for myself, I can see no point in teaching a farmer's lad about the Battle of Marathon. The Battle of Blenheim, now that's a different matter entirely. But as I say, all that is for you to decide and to justify and to defend *if*, as I say *if* you choose to take up my offer."

After that he explained the other details: the expectations of the Trustees - that the boys with their parents should attend church regularly, be prepared for confirmation and be instructed in what he vaguely described as 'the whole duty of man.' As for the master, it appeared that something akin to sainthood was expected from him. Expressions such as 'sober living', 'humble behaviour', 'meek temper' and 'good self-governance' were spoken of. Oh, and 'a genius for teaching.' I must admit, had I given these demands my full consideration at the time, I would have been utterly intimidated.

The business at an end, we made our way back to the

Woolpack to begin our journey home. That was as much as was said on the matter that day. We travelled all the way back to Stonham together and Candler uttered not another word on the subject of charity schools. It was turning dark before we came within sight of home. I found myself wondering as we parted company that evening if I had imagined the whole thing.

Part One

Chapter 1 ~ August 1763

It is early morning on Middlewood Green. Not really early morning by his standards - most men are still tucked up tight in their beds when the likes of Tiso Heron gets about. But opportunities offer themselves to the early riser. Tiso is what many would describe as an Egyptian, though this is probably about as far South as he has ever been in his life. He is of course a gipsy, and a familiar face in these parts at this time of year. Originally one of the Boswell clan, he has taken the name of his wife's family, for the Herons are better known here; both feared and respected. Though these are not the only names by which he has been known. Newly arrived the night before, he already has a fire started and is boiling water.

Only a small part of Middlewood Green is not enclosed - barely a widening of the dirt road leading to the Turnpike. Not much of a green; and as for the Middle Wood, that disappeared along with most of the other nearby woods to build Tudor ships, so they say.

So the Herons will not stay long, moving along to Forward Green or more likely down the hill beside the river where other travellers will join them to race their dogs and their horses or gather osiers for basket making.

At this time of day, there are snares to retrieve from the night before, along with other chance finds. It is not too late in the year to find water-hens' eggs or fetch down a sitting pigeon with a well-directed stone. There are herbs in the hedgerows - plantain to stop bleeding, tansy for gout, sticklewort for coughs and chamomile for flatulence. The list is endless, if you believe all the wise women say.

Above all, at this time of the year comes work - paid work.

There are never too many labourers when it is time to bring the harvest home. Early August has been wet in these parts and only now are the barley and beans and wheat ready. There will be money in their pockets and what is more, a gathering of the clans - the Lees, the Herons, the Smyths and the Days will be setting up their tents on the village greens and it will be a great social event. Some villagers will eye them with suspicion, but many will meet them as old friends. It is a time long-anticipated during the cold dark days of winter. A time to renew acquaintances, strike deals, tell stories, eat and drink and find husbands and wives for their daughters and sons. The most any nomad might hope for!

Tiso Heron sees the boy before the boy spots him. He looks familiar - a bit older than the last time perhaps: one of Thomas and Mary Brett's by the look of him. Probably young Tom. He is bending low, staring into the hedgerow, pulling at it.

"And what might 'ee be doin'?"

"Oh Mr Her'n, I'm gettin' a stick."

"An' how d'you reckon you'll be takin' it?"

"I'll snap it off," the boy grins.

"Not that'un you wun't."

"I'm stronger than last year. I'm seven and you know what - I'm goin' to school soon. I've been measured for the clothes an' all."

"I'm not denyin' you're a strong lad," says the gipsy. "But you'll not snap that stick. You'll see."

And he watches the boy bend the cane almost back on itself. But he is right; the cane doesn't snap.

"It's hazel you see. It don't break - not like ash. You'll more easily snap an ash cane, especially if you nick it first."

Then, pulling out a knife, he cuts into a different stick.

"You try it now"

Sure enough, the ash pole snaps clean off, to the boy's great satisfaction.

"So, you're goin' to school - down by the church is it?"

"Yes," young Tom says proudly, but then he pauses and looks a bit worried. "But some of the others have been at school last year. I'm new and they'll think I'm stupid."

"Now why should they think that when they was in the same position only a year or so ago - and what is more, I'll wager they don't know how to cut a stick from the hedgerow."

It is a long way for an seven year-old boy to walk daily from Middlewood Green to the opposite corner of the parish, but there are no boarders at Earl Stonham school and only when the snow is thickest on the wintry ground will he stay the night with the master and his family. As much as the learning, the exercise will make more of him and Tiso Heron can imagine it will be a very different lad he'll meet when he returns next summer.

But of course, the boy is right. His seven other classmates will think him stupid, or at least that's what they will say to begin with. Boys have very short memories. And likewise, young Tom will mock the next contingent of new boys in much the same way. The master, Mr. Warren will remind them all from time to time that they too had to start at the beginning in learning to read, casting accounts, answering questions from the Catechism; even writing their names.

By the time the school year begins in mid-September, the harvest is well underway and what amounts to a small gipsy encampment is well established just across the Lady Bridge beside the stream. The water is clear and pure and a couple of furlongs of race-course stretches out behind. There will be races for men, horses and dogs while they are there. It isn't like Newmarket Heath or even Bungay Common, but they take their racing seriously. Local landowners offer prizes. One of Tiso Heron's proudest possessions is a hat laced with gold that he won as young man riding the finest pony he ever owned. The shortness of the course means galloping and cornering sharply a number of times. It is a young man's sport. No longer a youth, Tiso will have to put his faith in his latest acquisition, a greyhound. A long lean animal, it is like lightning over a short distance and this year, his hopes are up.

The gipsy camp is much the same from one year to the next. As time goes on, a few die and a few replace them, but rarely is seen a new face entirely. This year is different. Regan is not of their kind. That is clear. His skin is paler. He is used to living out of doors, clear enough, but he does not speak the way they do and he doesn't understand the patois they use. For all that, he is not the kind of person you would feel comfortable telling that he isn't welcome. So the families tolerate the sullen newcomer, suspecting there is a story they will uncover one night over a bottle or two of strong liquor.

There is a story, of course; several stories if you believe all that was ever spoken of Morgan. For that is his real name, or at least the name the authorities seek him by. But even strong liquor fails to loosen his tongue to his neighbours. It will be a schoolboy who uncovers the colourful life of Morgan: the man who justifiably claims to be the luckiest man in all England.

Gleaning is a long-established tradition in the Suffolk countryside. Though not enshrined in law and denied in a number of parishes, Earl Stonham continues to accept that it is a way of helping their poorest to help themselves. For this reason, most are excluded from the practice. No-one from outside the parish, not even those across the turnpike in Stonham Aspal are allowed in Earl Stonham fields after harvest. Gipsies and other visitors are also barred from gleaning. Men, women and boys of working age and also those who have accepted a position in the charity school are forbidden to glean. This leaves only the elderly, nursing mothers, and tiny children. Even those unfit through a disability to work are considered by definition unfit to glean. Young Tom Brett will not be entering the gleaning fields as he did in previous years. No help to be had there; just one of the disadvantages of sending your child to school.

His mother and his younger siblings will glean from when the church bell tolls in early morning until it again reminds the poor of the parish it is time to take the little they have found and be thankful.

The poor: now there's an expression to be reckoned with. As if such a monumentally large phenomenon could be talked about as one. Even the most critical observers would hardly believe that. Thomas Warren the schoolmaster certainly doesn't. Even Candler Bird and the feoffees responsible for the distribution of charitable offerings make a distinction between the deserving poor and the undeserving and undesirable others. To them, there will always be a world of difference between the two.

The parish is spread wide, and in places you can do little more than imagine the ringing of bells. Today however, the wheat has been carted from the fields above the Church Mead. This means that Mary Brett can walk her son both to school and home again, a luxury that will not occur very often. Young Tom Brett walks with his mother from their home on Middlewood Green along the network of footpaths above the church to the old Guildhall which is now both home and workplace to Thomas Warren and his family.

The boy Tom is encased in his stiff new grey coat and other clothes purchased by the parish at the immense cost of nearly two pounds. He is already aware of the responsibility this lays upon him. What if he cannot learn? What if he really is stupid? For the next three years he knows he must make the most of this opportunity, after which he may be apprenticed at further expense to the parish to learn a trade that will set him up for life. He should be truly grateful. He knows that; but right now all he can feel is terrified.

In a field up the hill just below the Rectory, Tom's mother, Mary Brett and her colleagues are finding their activities less than productive. Either the harvesters have been more thorough than usual or someone has been there before them. With a gipsy encampment at the foot of the hill, the latter seems more likely. Hand-querning is a slow laborious process, but gipsy children are born to it and the flour for their flat bread certainly has to come from somewhere. There are mutters and moans. But in a day or two, they'll be away to the other side of the parish and hope for better results.

Inside the old Guildhall, Thomas Warren looks at his new class. Some of them seem very young indeed, but these are early days and time will tell what he can make of them. Just two remain from the previous year. George Buckle and Henry Robinson have been at the school for a year. The other six are beginners. Already, one of these boys stands out from the rest. Jerry Sharman is ten years old and has a way with numbers. He will struggle to read with the rest, but can already add columns of figures as fast as his teacher can write them down.

The other new boys are younger. Tom Brett and Isaac Pawsey are still just seven years old. Sam Tricker, James Nunn and John Coats are eight or thereabouts. Most are shy and serious. Only the Pawsey boy shows any spirit: doubtless the others will in time grow in confidence.

The master is concentrating on the new children. If his own wife was a little more literate and less concerned with their own two infants, she might be able to help in the schoolroom. But her education has been minimal: George Buckle, now starting his second year at the school, reads far better than she does.

"Mr. Warren, sir, how might I map the race course?"

Thomas Warren looks up. He likes George Buckle who has

taken to education with ability and enthusiasm. He is glad to have him back for another year. So many leave and start a job just as they are beginning to grasp reading and writing. He has to wonder how many retain it. He suspects that most of his boys, after leaving school, never open a book again.

"Let me spend a little longer with young Tom here and I'll get out the chains and show you."

Clearly George has been talking to the gipsies - maybe showing off a little in front of the Lee boys, claiming he has learnt more than he he actually knows.

George Buckle returns to the monitorial task he has been given, that of coaching three other boys on the Catechism. It is dull for a lad like him; the adventurous one of the group. But he knows that the master will keep his promise and he will be seen later that day measuring the narrow strip of land that for some odd reason belongs to their parish when all the other land on that side of the stream does not. George Buckle, more than most, values the education his village provides. He can see a day when he will travel the world and maybe even use his mapping skills on foreign shores.

The Catechism is not the most inspiring part of the Prayer Book. A set of rhetorical questions requiring little debate and less understanding. Casting his eyes over the eight young lads, full of mischief as ever, Thomas Warren can never quite imagine any one of them aspiring to *inner spiritual grace...* but then, you never can tell.

And they will learn their lines as they always do. Their parents will be proud and the Rector, Jeremy Pemberton M.A. (Cantab), may even tear himself away from his lucrative Girton parish and appear in Earl Stonham for their confirmation. Failing that, this work like most ecclesiastical duties in the parish, will be performed adequately by the Curate, Mr. Syer. For this and all his many duties, the Rev. Syer will receive not a penny of the tithes;

merely £30 per annum and a cold corner of the Rectory to call his own... in the hope that sooner or later, he will convince a sponsor of his suitability to benefit from a rectorial position.

Were it his school, Thomas Warren would by choice do things rather differently. But money is not readily available for any great quantity of pens and paper, except for those boys skilled enough to use them perfectly. It would not be a bad idea to teach the boys to turn chair legs or to darn socks. Such skills could even be turned into a profitable venture. He has heard of schools where this has been the case, but buying needles and yarn seems to be outside the Trustees' interest. He would relish the chance to show the boys pictures of the wider world, but after six years in the job, his own limited library is beginning to suffer, becoming torn and dog-eared. On his meagre salary there is little chance of improving it.

That above all is what really angers him. Candler Bird was apologetic enough at the outset regarding the eight pounds a year he was to be paid. In six years it has remained the same, as it had done for sixty years before that. To begin with, Warren didn't understand why. Now he has had a chance to view the accounts, he can see perfectly well why. His salary and all provision for the school is dependent on the rents collected for Halefield, Blunts, Dunhams and a few other assorted patches of land. What is quite clear is that these are let at a rate well below what might be expected on the open market. The Trustees cannot lease land to themselves. That would be improper. Instead they let those few acres that are their responsibility to their friends at advantageous rents and these same friends who are the Trustees of other charities return the favour. It is all rather incestuous and it has been going on here for a very long time. At the end of the day there is no-one to complain to. Candler Bird and his friends have it comfortably organised to the benefit of no-one but themselves.

There is a position he has considered making an application

for - that of Master of the Free Grammar School at Botesdale. But Thomas Warren knows he is poorly qualified for such a post and besides, it would undoubtedly mean exchanging one set of corrupt Trustees for another. No, for the time being, he will give of his best to the boys, and keep his suspicions to himself.

At one side of the room which doubles as a classroom and his own living space, he has constructed a large sand tray. Long before pens and ink are issued, boys trace letters in the moist sand. But boys will be the way boys are, and someone has drawn certain shapes in the sand whilst his back has been turned. With only eight boys to choose from, it isn't hard to identify the culprit. It is Isaac Pawsey. It usually is. And his brother had been such a nice lad. Unfortunately, this one would prefer to waste time - both his own and that of others. But he won't beat him - not this time. Just erase the poorly executed art-work and send the boy to the church to pray for forgiveness whilst he unlocks the coffer that holds his measuring chains.

Then leaving the errant child behind, he will lead the other seven over the roadway towards the rickety wooden bridge beside the ford. The weather is now warm and dry as it has been for over a week. The water is low and some of the boys choose to walk through rather than over. Acknowledging some of the gipsies, as they pass, Thomas Warren shows his class how to lay out the chains. At corners of the long water meadow, he erects posts with flat boards atop and checks, using strings with weights attached, that they are upright. With pins on the boards, he shows them how to calculate angles. Then, sacrificing one precious piece of paper, he proceeds to demonstrate how the shape on the ground might be transported in miniature to the plan he is drawing. It is almost mystical. Some of the gipsies have come to see for themselves and it is clear they are impressed, even though they cannot understand why he is doing it at all.

"Mr. Warren, sir." It is Isaac Pawsey, pulling at his cuff.

“I don’t recall asking you to join us Isaac. To my mind, boys who abuse the privilege of a schooling should not expect to be included in pleasures such as this.”

“Please sir, there is something you ought to see. It was coming away and I picked at it a little and there’s more - lots more.”

By now they are all intrigued so, striving not to run, they progress back over the roadway past the schoolroom and up through the churchyard to the church porch. Isaac has left the door open wide and they all scramble in. Then they see it. High up above the side of the pew where the boy must have been sitting, the lime-wash has begun to peel away. Left to his own devices, the boy must have grown bored so, climbing as high on the seating as he could, he has rubbed at the plaster, only to reveal... colour.

Thomas Warren has been in a number of churches before. He has heard that once many had brightly coloured paintings on the walls, but he has never seen one. He knows that a century earlier, many such paintings were lime-washed over. Now after a wet harvest followed by a dry Indian Summer, the church of St. Mary the Virgin has begun to offer up one of her greatest secrets.

“Should we rub some more off sir?” asks one of the boys. Isaac Pawsey starts to climb onto the pew end to demonstrate how it might be further revealed.

Warren is more cautious.

“No, leave it, you might take off the paint as well as the peeling plaster.” But already they can see details - a face, the tail of a mysterious and mythical beast, perhaps even a crown of thorns. And for once even Isaac Pawsey is silenced, lost in awe at the remarkable discovery he has made.

Just seven days later, the Earl Stonham Curate, Mr. Dye Syer is preparing for the return of the Rector. It is a task not quite as demanding as a visit from the Bishop, but very nearly. The

Rectory has in his absence been 'put to sleep' under a smothering of dust-sheets. Now windows have been flung open wide, beds aired, furniture dusted down and occasional employees have been sent for. Orders have been put to tradesmen to enable larders to be stocked. No-one knows how long Rev. Pemberton will be staying this time: but long enough to view what has been revealed and make a decision regarding what is to be done.

The first carriages to reach Stonham include none of the family - Cambridge servants to check all is well before their master arrives. It is a stiff climb up the hill from the church to the Rectory and they have to borrow a trace-horse or two to make the final ascent.

An hour or two later when Jeremy Pemberton and the family reach the church, they park their carriage in front and they all make their way up the path to view what has been revealed. Intent on making their way inside, they fail to even cast so much as a glance around them. Were they to know the efforts that have been made on their behalf, they might have taken more notice, but probably not. The churchyard grass has been clipped, first by tethered sheep, then painstakingly shorn with hand-shears. The paths shine white with freshly laid unblemished gravel. The fine old pargeted house at the edge of the graveyard has had a coat of pink wash. Flags fly from the church tower and a line of respectful schoolboys stand to attention beside the porch. All go unnoticed by the rector who is far more intent on seeing for himself what all the fuss is about.

Once inside, the Pembertons have first to adjust their eyes. It is a bright day out there and a whole lot dimmer in the church. Unable to resist, churchwardens and others have picked at the lime-wash further and more is to be seen and identified. Someone has climbed up high on the wall of the South transept and revealed much of what appears to be St. George slaying the dragon. Other designs look like the patterns found on ancient tiled floors. There is a nativity scene and altogether darker stories emerging from the peeling paint.

In the end, the rector's decision is to cover it all up again. There are those in the parish who find this hard to swallow, but doubtless, the Reverend has seen finer wall paintings in the vicinity of Pembroke College and besides, it must have been the decision of one of his ancestors to paint it over in the first place. He can hardly go against his own family even if it was to appease Oliver Cromwell and his puritanical vandals. Within a few days, fresh white walls are all there are to show for a lot of sound and fury. The caravan of coaches heads back west and the larger part of the rectory is tucked back under dust-covers. The only benefit to the curate is a pantry full of food that cannot be allowed to go to waste.

Chapter 2 ~ October 1763

Jacob Sharman's mother Elizabeth has a secret. Her son is receiving an education that he may not be entitled to. She has been keeping quiet about it for some time and it weighs heavy on her. Like Mary Brett, when possible she likes to walk her son to school. Often it is possible, as she works at Deerbolts Hall. Once the ancient seat of the Driver family, the mansion is now in a poor state and only occupied as often as when the few surviving elderly family members choose to visit. Unlike the rectory, it is not closed up for months on end. A small but dedicated team of retainers keeps the house warm and dry in winter, using the summer months to patch and mend what is now a sad reminder of a formerly great house.

It is said that long ago, a manor house stood here in the days when noble knights and their ladies gave the name 'Earl' to what was merely Stonham. Then the father of Thomas Driver, High Sheriff for the county, demolished it and put in its place a grand edifice. Since that time its grandeur has faded somewhat and, despite the best efforts of Elizabeth Sharman and her colleagues, it will need a new impetus to restore Deerbolts Hall to the way it was.

All this is supposition and as usual nobody is sure quite how much is history and how much is hearsay. Besides, crumbling cornices and pitted pediments are not what are foremost in Elizabeth Sharman's mind as she climbs the hill between the road and her place of work. No, it is her secret that occupies all her thinking moments right now.

It is over three months since her husband Thomas last came to the parish church with her on a Sunday, and people are beginning to notice. 'Has he found another woman to occupy his time?' they ask behind hands in front of lips. If only he had, it might not be so bad. Instead, his Sunday mornings involve more furtive behaviour just across the parish boundary in Mendlesham.

In a house still remembered as 'Duncans' where, a hundred years ago, hides were tanned in rancid pits filled with cattle urine and oak bark, Thomas Sharman now goes to meet with a brotherhood of friends. As far as Elizabeth can tell, they do nothing worse than pray and discuss the Bible. But these Quakers, as they are called in an attempt by others to ridicule them, are looked upon with suspicion and contempt. They have no priests to tell them what to think and this is dangerous and subversive in the eyes of the established church. What they do profess to believe collectively flies in the face of contemporary wisdom. They profess pacifism, would abolish the slave trade and see no reason why those amongst them with land and wealth should pay tithes to a church they would not wish to belong to.

And yet their son Jacob, known by all as Jerry, studies at the school. He wears the clothes the parish has provided. He is to be confirmed into their church - that is to say, her church. The parish has been good to them. Her sister's child has, only a month earlier, been buried at their expense. And it wasn't the poorest of pauper's burials. They don't ask for much in return. Loyalty perhaps. Elizabeth Sharman knows her husband's movements cannot go unnoticed for long. Then what?

It is a troubled lady who climbs the hill, moving from the water meadows in the valley to the stubble above and on to Deerbolts Hall. She has been married for nearly twenty years and now feels she hardly knows the man.

A carriage is parked outside in the front drive. That is something of a surprise. Months can go by at Deerbolts with few visitors. So what is afoot?

Candler Bird is there with his eldest son Samuel. There is quite a cluster of people around him. Elizabeth can recognise

Robert Driver and Mrs. Bugg the Housekeeper. There is a lot of chatter and it is hard to work out what is going on. Mrs. Bugg takes Elizabeth Sharman to one side.

"The Birds are moving into Deerbolts."

"What about old Mrs. Driver?" Elizabeth asks.

"She is rarely here now and will continue to live with her daughter. She will keep an apartment here for when she wishes to visit. In many ways it won't make a lot of difference for her, but we shall have to get used to a different master now, even if he is only a tenant."

You only have to look at Candler Bird to sense his delight. His family has risen in just three generations from the lowliest of yeoman farmers to occupying the finest house in the district.

Not that you'd know from its situation that it was an Earl Stonham house. Barely visible from any part of its own parish, it sits apart, only reached by road or track from Creeting All Saints. As if whoever lived there might want to divorce himself entirely from where he once belonged. Candler Bird and his son after him will occupy a demesne that is a separate corner of England, enjoying the splendours of manorial life and all that carries with it.

"Now we have to clean like we have never cleaned before, so His Lordship Mr. Bird knows what good staff he has, just in case he thinks he can find better," Mrs. Bugg informs her. For the meantime, Elizabeth Sharman's little problem will have to wait. She at least knows her duty.

It might present a somewhat crumbling facade, but by the time Candler Bird and his young family move in, every parapet and pediment, every bracket and balustrade, every finial and fanlight, in fact every last inch of the ornate interior has been scrubbed and dusted within an inch of its life. From within Deerbolts Hall, the view presents an outlook like few others. Masked by ancient elms and spreading chestnuts, the nearby

Turnpike is effectively screened. A mere too large to call a pond, yet hardly a lake, dominates the view from the front. A couple of pollarded willows and one solitary mature cedar are its only companions. Hornbeam and hazel, oak, ash and hawthorn serve as backdrop at the rear. Though the house is three storeys tall and stands close to the brow of the the hill that divides it from its Earl Stonham neighbours, it is masked by woodland - just enough woodland to justify the existence of a keeper's cottage tucked in amongst the trees. The only way of catching sight of Deerbolts Hall from Earl Stonham is to climb the church tower. Seclusion is the word you might use.

Were it his own, Candler Bird would probably remodel the place, but that is beyond even his ambition. Merely to live there will be enough. It will take time to acquire a sufficiency of the right kind of furniture, but already he feels like a Lord.

Together with the house and its land, he will be increasing his acreage. There is a cluster of barns and out-buildings set around a yard. There is stabling and a carriage-house and, down by the mere, a log shed housing a small boat. The mere is largely free of bird life. The summer birds of the water margins have disappeared and the winter ducks and geese have yet to show their faces. As if in anticipation, at one side the mere narrows to a point and is beset by a duck decoy. On the grassy slope leading down to the water's edge, eldest son Samuel is leading five of his siblings down to the boat-house to try out boating. Their anxious heavily-pregnant mother Mary looks on in some trepidation, wondering what she would do if one of them got into difficulties. Fortunately, sixteen year-old Samuel is keeping a watchful eye on them all. This will be Mary Bird's eighth pregnancy and she can do without the worry and the upheaval the move has caused. She is thirty-five years old and it seems as if she has been pregnant all of her life. She only baptised the latest one nine months ago. Though her husband is a generation older, she looks and feels senior to him. Having spent her first twenty years growing up in the town of Ipswich, she has never quite come to terms with being a farmer's wife and all that entails. Now she will be expected to become more of a Lady of the Manor. Candler is a Churchwarden, Overseer of the Poor; one of the Great and Good of the parish. She should be proud, but right now all she feels is tired.

Within a week, the latest child will be still-born, too early, too feeble even to draw breath. No life, no funeral. No real grieving. She has known as much before. When her first daughter died, she had been through it all - birth and baptism and burial over and past in a matter of days. Her Mary, named after herself of course. And even after time had healed the sorrow enough to enable her to give another daughter the same name, the pain had never really gone away. It is different this time. The Lord has taken away what the Lord has given and life must go on. There is a family to nurture and a position to fill in the parish. Candler says so.

Already, there is talk of Christmas. It is weeks away but there is so much to prepare even from her convalescent bed. Mrs. Bugg fortunately has it all in order. Mary Bird likes Mrs. Bugg. She is a typical Suffolk no-nonsense sort of woman. Swarthy looking, she has a permanent air of busy-ness. Like most of the staff, she hails from one of the Creeting villages. Though she has a small cottage of her own half a mile away, much of the time she prefers to occupy a room in the attic from which she can work long and hard, demanding the same devotion from everyone else. It is an admirable arrangement.

The larger family will come to visit this year - Candler's brother John and his wife Sarah with their children. There will also be some from his mother's side though they have been led to believe that Mary's family are unlikely to make the trek from Ipswich. It all means planning. But Mrs. Bugg is not concerned. If she can again prove her value, she will feel all the more secure.

"Mrs Bugg, could I speak to you please?" It is Elizabeth Sharman.

"Yes, of course my dear, what is it?"

"Not here - somewhere private."

The two servants are standing in the hallway. Most of the family are out. Mr. Bird is somewhere around the farm, the three boys are at school. The girls are with their aunt and baby Deborah is in the nursery. Mrs. Bird is still in bed. Sensing this might be important Mrs. Bugg hustles them both into the empty dining-room.

"We'll not be disturbed here."

"It's..." She stutters and pauses and stutters again. "You won't repeat what I say to you to anyone else, will you?"

"I promise you whatever is bothering you won't be bothering anybody but me. But if you have a problem then we can work it out between us. Is it that man of yours?" she asks as if all the problems of the world stem from the male sex.

"Yes, in a way it is. I don't see how I can really complain. He's a good man. He thinks of me and the children. He thinks about how to make the world a better place for us - that's the problem. All this thinking and it might be better for all of us if he just had a drink or two like everybody else's husband and forgot his thinking for a while. If I knew he was supping an ale at the Angel it wouldn't be so bad, but he's given all that up you see."

"So what are you complaining about? He sounds like a saint."

"It's those friends of his," cries Elizabeth. The tears really are beginning to flow now. "That's it... the Brotherhood of Friends they call themselves - meet over at the old tannery at Mendlesham. If Mr. Bird finds out I'll lose my job, Jerry'll lose his place in the school; who knows what will happen to Thomas and his job on the farm - we'll be thrown out of our home and all because he joins some silly Bible group. I'm too old to start all over again."

"These men! Either they just don't think or they think a lot more than is good for them. The way I see it, you have a secret and it needs to stay a secret?" says Mrs. Bugg.

"All this secrecy - it's too much."

"Are there others who know about this?"

"I don't rightly know - somebody must have seen him walking there three times a week."

"Then someone else is keeping that secret," Mrs. Bugg says comfortingly. "Look at it this way. Mr. Candler Bird now lives about as far away from that side of the parish as he could. The other leading gentry are living up on Forward Green. Unless someone you know goes out of their way to cause trouble, I don't see how this can get to be anyone's concern but your own. So you dry your tears and give me a hand with turning the mattresses for the last time before the Spring."

And that is that. Having shared her problem, Elizabeth Sharman now feels less alone with it. Though nothing has changed and nothing has been done about it, at least the problem has been shelved, for the time being.

Over the hill and down the other side, her youngest son is blissfully unaware of any of this. He is learning well. The master Mr. Warren is pleased with him and has promised to show him how to write his name. Unfortunately, Mr. Warren has been, like every one else, calling him Jerry. He doesn't realise the boy's name is Jacob and has assumed he was christened Jeremiah. Never mind, it's only three more letters. That is something else he has learned.

Jerry Sharman's mother will time her leaving work at the Hall to coincide more or less with her boy's finishing his school day. As she descends Church Field, she can see that the gipsy camp that has been there for a month or more has gone. The Herons and the Smyths, the Lees and the Marjorams have moved on to wherever it is they go next. Only one tent remains and it is there Elizabeth Sharman finds her son, along with Tom Brett, in earnest conversation with the one remaining camper, the man they know as Regan.

Never quite telling them the whole truth, the man others seek as Morgan has explained how he considers himself the luckiest man alive. He has certainly seen life, has Morgan. And he has been mighty close to death on a number of occasions, which is probably what makes him more reckless than most. Still, he has waited until others have departed, in the knowledge that he will too, after telling these lads just why he believes he is blessed.

Elizabeth Sharman joins them as he tells his tale, and a good tale it is, if one is to believe the half of it.

"You know what the inside of a gaol is like?"

The boys shake their heads.

"You don't want to know. Leastways not the gaol I was banged up in. Newgate. Condemned to death. There's a place to make your blood run cold. And no sooner do I get there than some fool sets the place alight. Locked in and chained up as a fire blazed around me. I was making my peace and preparing to meet my maker, I can tell you. And still I didn't die. Instead, I wrenched free taking my chains with me. But they caught me and took me back to court. Condemned I was again for trying to escape. I told 'em, 'what's a man supposed to do when there is smoke and flame all around?' And they said, 'we'll transport you instead to Philadelphia.' Have you heard what the Indians are doin' to folks in Philadelphia? Scalpin' 'em and roastin' 'em. But that was where I was sent - across the water to New York and upriver to Philadelphia."

"Weren't you terrified?" asks Tom Brett.

"Oh ay, but there was worse to come. On the journey that boat sprang a leak, but rather than let me drown they undoes my chains so I leaps over the side and swims to the far shore."

"Was it very wide that river?" asks Jerry Sharman.

"As wide as from here to that there church I'd say."

The boys gasp. It seems an immense distance. They can't imagine any river could be that wide.

"And I found my way back to New York. Of course there were all sorts of dangers along the way, but as I said, I'm the luckiest man alive. Then no sooner had I found a ship bound for home, than someone saw my number."

At this he peels back his sleeve to reveal a roughly branded number on his forearm.

"So I was taken, you see, for trying to return from a sentence of transportation, and you know what the penalty for that is?"

"Is it death?"

"That it is - death by hanging. But the good Lord still didn't mean me to die. Again I broke free from my cell and vanished over the rooftops."

"Why did they arrest you in the first place?" asks Elizabeth, intrigued by the tale every bit as much as the two boys.

"Now there's a whole other set of stories. Shall we just say I had a way back then of helping separate rich travellers from their belongings."

"Are they still looking for you?" asks Tom Brett.

"That they are, but you wouldn't tell 'em you'd seen me, now would you boys... or you missus?"

They all shake their heads, but whether from loyalty or from fear it is hard to say.

"And that is just a part of my story. When I'm gone, they will know I was here, but by then it will be too late. I shall be somewhere else. And in probability, I shall be some*body* else."

Sensing oncoming darkness, Elizabeth Sharman begins the walk home with two boys chattering away fired with excitement by the tale they have just heard.

The following day, that tent too is gone. But constables

have been called to the Toll House up the road beside the Turnpike. During the night, someone has held up the gatekeeper at pistol-point and stolen the money collected from tolls that day, along with a horse. Two small boys, when they hear about it, have little doubt who was responsible.

But they say nothing.

Chapter 3 ~ Christmas 1763

People can better themselves. That, one might suppose, is the whole purpose of the exercise. Education, that is. Ironically, it could be suggested that of the class of '63, the one making the least progress with his life may well have turned out to be the master, Thomas Warren. A fat lot of good his education seems to have done him in the first thirty-one years of his life. A pitifully paid job instructing the sons of the poor in the vain hope they may find a use for such as he sees fit to teach them.

Also he finds himself smothered within a marriage that was not made in heaven. She seemed pleasant enough when he coaxed her away from a bullying father, but now she has her life built around her two infants - and they seem very much to be *her* children. A distance has opened up between husband and wife. Which is why his eyes are beginning to wander.

Still he has found a way of involving her in his work. They are to perform a play for Christmas. He has begged some well-worn fabrics from John Coats' mother and, with a little help, Beth Warren has agreed to cut and sew them into the semblance of costumes.

The entertainment is to take the form of a miracle play such as might have been performed centuries before. There will be familiar characters such as the Devil, (that wasn't difficult to cast, was it Isaac Pawsey?) St. George (a little more difficult even if his name is George) and of course, a dragon. That will be the most challenging of the costumes.

With not too much moaning, Beth Warren will exercise her needlework skills with the help of one or two of the boys' mothers. Everyone is very excited. They have been talking of nothing else for weeks.

But then, these boys are quite a capable group. Surprisingly so. Probably the best class yet. And that may well be how they come to better themselves. At this time only one of the boys is not the son of an agricultural labourer. Eighty years from now, numbered amongst their ancestors will be bakers and shopkeepers, farmers and millers, smiths and engineers - oh, and the occasional criminal.

It is at this time that Martha Palmer enters their lives. It is all a little unexpected, but that's the way these things tend to happen. The Palmers are a respectable and respected family from Stonham Aspal. There is a distant family connection with John Coats' parents. John refers to her as his 'cousin', but it is all a bit more complicated than that.

John Coats' parents are the only ones sending a child to the school who don't actually live in the parish. Johnny is also the only one in the class not of labouring stock. His father John farms land just across the parish boundary in Stowupland. But it is part of the parcel of land left by the same benefactor responsible for the endowment of the school. Mr. Coats pays his dues to Stonham, so stands to benefit from the fact. As a result, this is another child whose journey each day is about as far as it could be and, because they are not labourers, he is brought there in a small but serviceable carriage. The youngest of seven children, Johnny is small for his age and a little slow to absorb new skills. So it is that his mother comes to help with the sewing group one December day, bringing with her an assistant, the fifteen year-old Martha Palmer.

Martha proves to be less than adept with a needle and thread so turns her attention to helping her cousin with his reading. At this she has more success and it becomes clear to all after a few days that she has a genuine talent as a teacher's assistant. Added to which she is pretty and petite and brings a sparkle to the dull environment of the old Guildhall that serves as the classroom.

And it is dull! Built some three hundred years earlier for a long-forgotten purpose, it is not the most inspiring of places to generate a child's enthusiasm. Desperately in need of repair, fresh leaks appear almost daily. They are beset by vermin in the thatch and in the walls. The only really solid part of the structure is the brick chimney, built as an afterthought. Situated down on the valley floor, it is poor at carrying away the smoke from the open hearth and the room has to be regularly ventilated by opening doors and windows, despite the cold outside. The Trustees have promised to do something about the problem, but their past record of action is such that nobody expects any kind of improvement to be made in a hurry.

Still, the boys take it in turns to sit nearer to the fire whilst the poor master Thomas Warren wraps another scarf around himself and hopes the interminable winter will not last too long. The one saving grace is the girl from Stonham Aspal who now seems to be a regular assistant in the classroom. Somehow her continued presence seems to have warmed the room up a bit.

Two of the boys, George Buckle and Henry Robinson have been studying at the school a year longer than the rest and are preparing for their confirmation. Others are learning to write their name. For some, this may be all the writing they will ever need. Even that may prove unnecessary when the time comes. Then they may feel it is more befitting their position to sign with a cross, as if writing their name was inappropriate. After all, signing means just what it says doesn't it: making the sign, not being grand and important and writing your name!

Martha Palmer flits from boy to boy checking how they are getting on. Some are using chalk or charcoal on a board, John Coats is finger-tracing in the sand tray. They repeat the task a number of times. Eventually, they may be allowed paper and pen but must prove first that their skill and concentration warrant it.

The schoolroom is quiet; so quiet they can hear the sewing group in the adjoining room talking and laughing together. The costumes are taking shape, and this afternoon they will try them on for the first time.

"Please Mr. Warren sir, is this how it should be. Could I try chalk and a board like the others?" John Coats is desperate not to seem different.

But he is different. Just as he is the only one brought to school in a carriage, only he has a second pair of breeches and stockings specially bought to match those supplied by the school's Trustees. If the other boys resent his slightly higher status, they have learned not to show it. After all their parents may well be like Sam Tricker's father at some time or another. Following the Michaelmas hiring, he now works for John Coats Snr. Next year, it could be someone else's father. You wouldn't want to get on the wrong side of a man your family might eventually become beholden to.

So, the timid boy who might easily have found himself bullied is safe. And anyway, Mr. Warren would have nothing but contempt for a bully. He has made himself abundantly clear about that. The odd thing is, such a thought probably wouldn't have crossed the minds of the boys in this class.

That is another thing about them. There is no bullying, no unnecessary unpleasantness. They have become a group, a team, almost a family. The older ones look after the younger ones. Not because they have been told to. This class, of all the classes he has taught, feels special. Thomas Warren can sense it. And there is nothing like a grand performance to make it even more special!

Just before Christmas time, the Mystery Play is performed in the parish church. They all come to see - the curate, the boys' parents, the siblings, the Trustees, a few past pupils and plenty of others who have merely come to find out what all the fuss is about. The rector does not attend. No-one has invited him. The thinking is that anyone who would cover over ancient wall-paintings would almost certainly not approve of an entertainment forbidden by the Church of England two centuries earlier (probably by another of the rector's ancestors).

Just days earlier, the master had been worrying about it all. The children had appeared so wooden. They had known their lines, but had given little life to their performance. Now as they put on the costumes, everything changes. Just as their grey school clothes have turned mere boys into students, so the costumes give confidence and purpose to their acting roles. Now, he knows, they will be performers. They will strut the stage and be everything that is expected of them. Even shy, quiet Samuel Tricker when placed inside the dragon suit will take on a part that is so far removed from his normal personna, even his proud parents will watch transfixed in disbelief.

Much is performed in tableaux with lines narrated by the older boys. But there are verses in rhyme that each child has learned by heart. Thomas Warren has selected only parts of the play that will appeal to the boys. They deliver their lines with gusto.

James Nunn, as the fairest among them, is the Angel...

> "I am favoured and fair and figured full fit;
> The form of all fairness upon me is fast.
> All wealth I am wielding, so wise is my wit;
> The beams of my brightness are built with the best"

And Isaac Pawsey makes a wonderful Devil...

> "Oh, helpless! so hot is it here.
> This is a dungeon of dole in which I am set.
> Where are my kin now, so comely and clear?
> Now am I loathliest, alas, where is light.
> My brightness is blackest of hue now;
> My blood is beating and burning,
> That makes me go grinding and grinning.
> I wallow enough in woe now."

And there is the added bonus of Martha Palmer who has

agreed to take on the female parts - Eve being turned out of the garden at the time of the creation, the maiden to be sacrificed to the dragon before St. George comes to her rescue, and Mary at the birth of Jesus.

Everyone leaves the church that night having enjoyed an entertainment the like of which has probably not been seen in Earl Stonham since the Guildhall was simply the Gild Hall.

And when George Buckle draws forth his sword to slay the dragon, people cheer. In church! They cheer! Loudly. It is just as well the rector is not here. He would not have approved. But everyone else does, and they go on talking about it until the winter is long past and blackthorn buds are beginning to burst white in the hedgerows.

Chapter 4 ~ April 1764

Everything you do in life is life-threatening. Mary Nunn knows this only too well. She has already buried two infants and a sister, and each time she packages her son James into his grey broadcloth coat and sends him off to school, she dreads the day he may not return. Much the same can be said of her attitude regarding her husband Joshua. Here she has already had cause for concern - the day he was kicked by a horse and for a week they all despaired of his recovery. But by the grace of a merciful God, he did recover. Then when he fell from a stack and narrowly avoided losing an eye, falling on a half-buried pitchfork! Still it doesn't get any easier. Everything, but everything may be life-threatening. Life is so transient, so fragile. A man can cut his hand on a flint and die a month later from the mortification. He can spend weeks threshing and fill his lungs with chaff until he can't breathe. He can fall victim to any one of a dozen killer diseases... children more than adults. Two of Mary Nunn's offspring have already succumbed to sweating-sickness and scarlatina. So when she reaches the end of each day with her family still safe and well, she falls to her knees to give thanks to God for delivering them this time.

More than most mothers, she sees dangers in all things. But James of all her children seems hale and healthy. He has the spirit of a typical nine year-old. He takes risks - not what he would describe as risks - but adventurous activities that, were she to know about them, would send his mother instantly to her knees praying for his deliverance.

Now it is warmer and the days are lengthening, some of the boys do not hurry home, especially those with shorter journeys to make. They look for ducks' nests along the river or pull sheep's wool from the thorn bushes. Some of them have rigged up a swing by plaiting hemp string a number of times into a form of rope and tying a stick to it to create a seat. James and his friend Henry Robinson are trying it out for the very first time.

"I'll sit on it and you pull me back so I can swing out over the stream," suggests Henry. He is a year and a bit older than James, so assumes he will have the first go.

After a few tries, he clambers off and the smaller boy, with some difficulty climbs aboard.

"Hey, I can see right up the river both ways," James calls as he swings around as well as across and back. He leans back, transferring his weight suddenly in one direction. The threads begin to give way and he is plunged down into the water, cutting his head on a stone embedded in the clay bank. There is an awful lot of blood. The stream turns red for quite a distance and for a moment, Henry is unsure what to do. Hauling the moaning boy out of the cold water, he leaves him dazed and whimpering on the bank whilst he runs for help across the road to the school. The master: Mr. Warren - he will know what to do.

He has chosen a bit of a bad moment. He can hear voices raised in the schoolroom. Mrs. Warren is really letting rip. Her own two children clinging to her, she is not happy. She is definitely not happy!

"Every time she comes into this room, you go all doe-eyed. She's a child for heaven's sake. But everyone can see you are lusting after her," she screams.

"I don't know what you are talking about. She comes to help twice a week at most. And she *is* a help. The boys like her and learn better when she is there to give me support." Thomas Warren is trying to placate her, but it is clear she is having none of it.

"Look at the way she dresses. You must be able to see that it is provocative - deliberately provocative," she continues.

"It is getting warmer. We are all shedding a few layers at last."

"A few layers! As if that was all. Well, I'll tell you now, you are to inform her she is no longer needed. You can send a letter then she needn't come again."

"I will do nothing of the sort. I am the master here, both in my house and in my school. I need help. You are unable to give it. She will continue to be my assistant."

That was a low blow. Beth Warren is aware she is poorly educated. Her reading is poor and her writing non-existent. If he insists on having an assistant, she knows it cannot be her.

"Then find someone else: preferably someone less comely."

"Don't be a fool woman. Who would come and do what she does for no payment. She will doubtless leave when her cousin takes up an apprenticeship. But in the meantime, she stays whether you like it or not!"

Beth Warren can see this is one battle she will not win, but she leaves him a parting thought.

"All right, if you must, but I'm warning you, I'm keeping my eyes on the pair of you and if anything untoward comes to my attention, then her father will be the first to know about it."

Outside the door, intrigued by what he has been hearing, but still concerned for his friend, Henry Robinson seizes on a pause in the conversation to tell the master of the problem.

Within minutes, Thomas Warren is across the road, over the rickety bridge and down the bank where the remains of the boys' swing hangs above. James is even paler in complexion than usual, the fair hair on one side of his head stained bright red. There is blood; quite a lot of it, but the schoolmaster has seen enough boys' injuries to know that head grazes often look worse than they really are. He carries James Nunn back to the schoolroom where he and his wife in an apparent act of togetherness patch the boy's wound and ensure he is returned to his over-protective mother in slightly better shape than he had been half an hour earlier. Her response is predictable. Mary Nunn fusses like they knew she would. There will be extra prayers of thanks tonight.

The following day, She keeps her son at home. Just to be on the safe side, she says, though there seems little wrong with him beyond the band of cloth wound around his head. Henry Robinson ensures the other boys all know every word of what he has heard at the schoolroom door the night before. Even John Coats has to chuckle. And a day or two later when Martha Palmer comes again to help, the smirks thinly concealed behind the boys' hands make it clear to Thomas Warren that it will not only be his wife who will be watching him from now on.

Occasionally journals will come their way - discarded copies of the Gentleman's Magazine or, more commonly, issues of the Ipswich Journal. Thomas Warren does not subscribe to these organs himself. Even if he could afford it, two and a half pence weekly for a voice-piece of Tory propaganda seems an unnecessary expense, especially as most of the information printed is a digest of accounts published a week earlier in the London papers. Usually these well-thumbed copies arrive at the school courtesy of the grander houses in the area, often by way of local hostelries.

As the boys' reading proficiency increases, they find items, usually of a more shocking nature, to read and entertain them. It is an encouragement to the slower readers to have their colleagues read of Indian uprisings in America or skirmishes with the French in the Canadian provinces. There may be details relating to the King and the royal family or anecdotes to amuse and entertain inquiring minds. This week, they are reading of a small fat man, unable to pay his gambling debts at Newmarket, who has hanged himself in an outhouse. There is news of exotic animals being brought from Africa and presented to the Prince of Wales. There are stories of men and women condemned for murder and burglary and mutiny. And there are further exploits of Lord Clive in India. It is a good issue as far as the boys are concerned.

But after they have all gone home, it is one notice of advertisement that catches Thomas Warren's eye. Not that he is actually reading the paper. Casually folding it, he spots a familiar word or two halfway down the back page and stops to read it all more carefully.

WANTED IMMEDIATELY.

A MASTER to the FREE-SCHOOL of MENDLESHAM in Suffolk, where twelve Boys are conſtantly to be taught gratis in Reading, Writing, and Arithmetick, and the Maſter muſt be qualified to teach the Latin Tongue, if required;---but be it noted, that no Perſon who is not extremely well verſed in Arithmetick, and quite Maſter of his Pen in Writing, will be accepted. The annual Salary of the School is Twenty Pounds, and the free Uſe of a fine ſpacious Room that will contain 50 Boys at leaſt, and where all due Encouragement will be given to a careful and induſtrious Man.---It muſt be a Perſon that is brought up in the Church of England, and can come well recommended for his Morals and good Behaviour.

For Particulars enquire of Mr. Brown, Attorney at Law, at Ipſwich; of Mr. Marriott, Attorney at Law, at Stow-upland; or the Rev. Mr. Chilton of Mendleſham.

It is the sense of urgency that attracts his attention. They have been left wanting by a master who has abandoned his class mid-year. Barely three miles away, a similar charity to the one he now serves is offering more than double what he receives from Stonham. Added to which there is every indication he could supplement his income further by taking in fee-paying students. It seems too good an opportunity to miss. Admittedly his Latin is not all it might be, but it is unlikely anyone is going to inquire too closely about that. Fortunately they are not demanding someone who has had the smallpox.

For the next two days his attention is distracted as he mentally composes the letter of application he intends to write. He tells his wife of his intention and she too seems excited by the prospect. The letter takes a further three days to write. With it in his hand, walking as far as the Turnpike, he tries first the Brewery Tap, then the Angel, before he finds a man prepared for a fee to convey it to the Rev. Mr. Chilton at Mendlesham. After which, he waits.

Several weeks pass with the same advertisement still appearing in the Ipswich Journal. He begins to wonder whether his letter of application was ever delivered. Then he does know.

Candler Bird drives up in his gig just as school is beginning for the day. That is a surprise in itself. Since his move up and over the hill, he has not been seen in the parish a great deal. Some say he has taken to attending church at Creeting where people raise their hats to him. He stands at the open door to the schoolroom, sporting a new peruke; so new that the powder is whitening his jacket shoulders. It is a bright and a lovely morning. Thomas can see he is clutching a letter.

"I have received a correspondence," he begins. "It appears you are not content here."

"It is not that," Thomas replies. "I struggle to maintain a family on the remuneration I receive, as you well know."

There is a pause, so he continues. "Following my work here, which appears to have been satisfactory, I hope you will see your way to lending support to my application."

Again there is a pause, then...

"I think I may have a small problem with that."

"But surely..."

"I think if you study the wording of the notice in the Journal..." Here he proffers a copy of the paper for May 19th. "...you will read." He points to the last line relating to the description. "We have some concern..." he says as if using the Royal 'we', "...over your relationship with a certain young lady."

"Nothing untoward has happened!" His voice is raised and

heads are lifting from work inside the schoolroom.

"That's as maybe, but you understand my position. I have to give my word that you are a fit person to fulfil the role as described."

"If I am not fit to teach there, why do you continue to employ me here?"

"That, Thomas, has been a cause for concern, I can tell you. Mr. Coats is definitely concerned. But of course, beggars are not left with many choices and we can hardly abandon our own boys because of a little hearsay. On the other hand, offering our recommendation to others is a different matter entirely. I'm sure you understand."

With which, Candler Bird takes his leave. Back round to his grand house. Leaving the schoolmaster Thomas Warren speechless. The worst part is explaining to his wife Beth why he has been rejected. He says it is his lack of Latin and blames the Trustees for not being prepared to back him and land themselves with the problem of finding a replacement. But somehow in his resentment, he knows this is not the end of the matter. Not the end at all.

To take both of their minds off such matters, at the first opportunity Thomas and Beth and their two children arrange an excursion to Ipswich to see Mr. Pinchbeck's astronomical and musical clock, along with the waxworks being displayed there. Though they complain about the 6d charge for admission and agree that the waxworks are not in the least lifelike, it is a day they all enjoy.

A special coach has been commissioned, starting from the Pye Inn, just up the hill and along the road. It will pick up passengers at the crossroads by the Brewery Tap. It will not be a comfortable journey - it never is. Every bump in the road, and there are many, will be keenly felt by those aboard. The coachman is red-faced and foul-mouthed. He does not inspire confidence. His skin is that of a man used to being out in all weathers, but he already stinks of the liquid breakfast he has imbibed and his speech is slurred. He has a belly on him that comes from a diet of fat mutton stew only to be found on the menu at lower-class coaching inns. To travel as far as Ipswich without a change of horses will require a certain tact and consideration on the part of the driver. It seems unlikely that will be in evidence.

Beth claims to be fearful over the rumours of footpads and highway robbers along the road to Ipswich, but there is too much traffic to tempt all but the most desperate and intrepid of thieves that day. And besides, as he observes... "Anyone can see the occupants of this mean coach have few farthings to risk robbing."

Whilst there, he purchases a book: 'Every Man his own Physician,' by John Theobald. It is an expense they can ill afford, but as he says, it is the sort of book a good parent should own.

Chapter 5 ~ May 1764

The things people do for love! They make fools of themselves and those they ought to care for most; they risk or sacrifice everything they hold dear; some even resort to crimes so dire and dreadful that no punishment seems appalling enough.

They are still talking about Margery Beddingfield a year after the event. She gave up everything for love. And for the murder of her husband was given the most barbaric of sentences - to be dragged from the gaol at Ipswich on a sledge up to the heath, to watch her lover Richard Ringe as they hanged him slowly, using the shortest rope permitted: then to be burned alive before a crowd of thousands baying for her slow and dreadful death. For her crime was deemed worse than his. To murder your husband is a betrayal of trust so abominable it is still described as petty treason. An ancient crime with an ancient remedy. Dreadful indeed, though there are still plenty around who say she got no more than she truly deserved. Higgins, the carrier from Stonham Aspal claims to have been on Rushmere Heath that day and he says that they had tied her neck to the post so tight she was insensible by the time they burned her. It still seems barbaric to Thomas Warren who wonders what it would take to drive his wife to such desperate measures. But then it is not his wife whose eyes are wandering and looking lustfully elsewhere.

Beth Warren wants another child. And he has to admit motherhood does become her, but keeping just two infants on his meagre salary is hard enough and more to the point, it is not very often any more that they find themselves likely to bring about such an outcome. On the rare occasions he and his wife make love, it is not Beth Warren's face he is imagining in the throes of passion. And what is more, she knows it!

Neither of them mentions the matter. They keep their peace. But there are arrowed comments from both sides and it is an uneasy peace that prevails in the house.

It is not that Beth Warren is a bad wife. Quite the opposite. Many of her qualities are admirable. She keeps a comfortable home - as comfortable as their situation permits. She is a good mother. She fails to grasp much of what the role of a school-master entails, preferring to devote her attention to her growing children. They are, as are many in the parish, named after their parents: Thomas aged five and Elizabeth a year younger. The births of both were skilfully planned for the August recess. They are strong and healthy but a little timid, clinging close to their mother and avoiding their brooding father whenever possible.

As the school year moves towards a close, Thomas Warren begins to contemplate such changes as must come about in September. Fortunately these will be far fewer than usual. For the first and last time in his short career, the same eight boys will remain together and form the same class for a second year. He can't help but be pleased. Already they have formed themselves into a talented and formidable group. Eventually they will begin to splinter and who knows what the future will offer them. But for now the class of '63 will become whatever he can make of them.

Life in a village like Earl Stonham is largely predictable. There are good harvests and there are poorer ones, but there *are* harvests - at harvest time. There are deaths and newly-born infants. There are the rich who generally thrive and the poor who struggle but generally survive. Little changes. But just occasion-ally an event may offer up a talking point that takes conversation away from the cycle of existence and the seasons.

Early in July a young man is seen around the parish. He is not one of your usual travellers - too pale in his complexion. Noticed by a number of people, it is unclear where he is residing.

He is of a fair height: five foot eight or more and unwigged, with light brown hair that curls up over his collar. For the time of year, he seems overdressed, with a thick fustian frock-coat and a linen handkerchief tied around his neck. His waistcoat is of faded pink and green and he wears leather breeches. His pockets bulge and all manner of suggestions are offered as to why. Still for a few days, he is seen around the area by the local inhabitants. He looks suspicious and people take to locking their doors when they go out. Then, a piece of the church plate goes missing. It is an old communion cup - a little dented, so rarely used now except by way of decoration. It was there and now it's not. Nobody is in much doubt who has taken it. Now the hunt is on. After school, the boys and the master join a party to search all outlying farm buildings and unoccupied houses. One or two farmers have brought shot-guns - just in case. And they do find his lair - a makeshift shelter in a ditch tunnelled by bushes, dry enough at this time of year. But the man has gone, leaving behind a piece of black crepe and some tassels from an altar-cloth, thankfully not from Stonham Church.

The constables are informed and the parishioners learn they have had a lucky escape. It is none other than the notorious William Bacon of Diss. In all likelihood, the bulge in his pocket was a pistol. He is wanted in three counties for burglary and sacrilege. A week later, the boys are able to read how he has been taken at Ipswich Race Ground and committed to gaol, after which he is removed to Chelmsford Gaol on a charge of highway robbery. It doesn't take much imagination for them all to work out how this story will end.

Careful he may be, but Thomas Warren cannot rid his thoughts of Martha Palmer. Still once or twice a week she will appear and weave her magic on all in the schoolroom. John Coats will remain in the class for at least another year. That guarantees his pretty cousin will continue to play her part in his education.

Just before school closes for the harvesting, Martha arrives riding a small pony. She sits astride the horse, a move bound to scandalise those easily offended. Fortunately, she arrives early. Few occupied houses are close to the old Guildhall. A grandly pargeted messuage stands to one side of the churchyard, but the Brewes family who own it are rarely in attendance. So there are no onlookers to see her dismount. Even the master's wife, Beth Warren is away up the hill visiting her father, who is unwell. The master is there alone.

"You're very early," says Thomas.

"I thought I could be useful," she smiles. "Anything you'd like me to do I'll do. I don't mind what?"

This is all slightly unsettling, but not unpleasant.

"I thought I'd make up some ink. Sacrifice a little paper. See how well they can all write."

"I had hoped I might do something a bit more... special."

Thomas looks furtively around him. Fortunately; or unfortunately; nobody is there to hear. He can imagine what one or two of the older boys might assume if they had heard. He isn't quite sure of what *he* has heard. As he glances from a side window, away a furlong or so up the road he can see the first two boys making slowly for the school. It is Sam Tricker and Jerry Sharman. They are usually the first. Being the youngest and the last in their families, their mothers are free to work from an early hour.

As he stands watching, Thomas becomes aware of a breath on his neck, then a cheek pressed tight to his. Pulling him to one side of the window, Martha presses her lips to his and her body full against him. He can feel himself responding; and continues to do so until they can both hear voices coming closer. By the time the first two pupils arrive, the two already in the schoolroom are a picture of innocence, the master putting out Bibles for reading and his young assistant mixing the ingredients for ink.

Chapter 6 ~ October 1764

Isaac Pawsey is in trouble again. It isn't always his fault, but he is by nature feckless and therefore prone to ill-judged and ill-timed errant behaviour.

"It wun't me Mr. Warren, sir, It wun't."

"Unfortunately, Isaac, the evidence is all too plainly on your hands."

It is. Dark black stains of ink are there for all to see, matching those on two of the other boys' copy-books. In those lads' defence, they haven't complained, being prepared to accept the blame themselves. That is the nature of this class. They could have been left to sort it out for themselves. A unit. A united whole. 'Thomas Warren's boys'. That is how he views them these days. More-so than his own two children cuddling up to their mother in the next room. It is odd really, but he spends far more meaningful time with these eight boys than he has ever done with little Thomas and Elizabeth.

He has tried. He has even attempted to start to teach his six year-old son to read, but he cannot hold his interest. He doesn't usually have as much of a problem with the boys he teaches. Probably, he thinks, his son is too young. But as time goes on, he will realise it is more than that, and it will become clear it is a waste of both of their time.

He finds it hard to be cross with Isaac Pawsey, even if he is lying to try to save his own skin. So he adopts a different attitude. Teaching the same small group for so long, the master finds he is constantly searching for ideas to keep the class interested. Isaac Pawsey may be an occasional irritant, but he serves to remind Thomas Warren how easy it is for boredom to lead to misbehaviour. And he knows how easy it is for childhood misbehaviour to lead to a lifetime of petty crime. Beyond that, of course, matters can become increasingly problematic. So he adopts a rather different approach.

"Isaac, I have a job for you. I want you to go to the long barn at Deerbolts Hall and ask the gentleman you find there if he would be so kind as to pay us a visit."

Seven other faces are now raised from their work. What is all this about?

"In't you gonna cane him, sir?" That is Tom Brett.

Why he asks, the schoolmaster cannot think. A cane does still hang on the inside of the schoolroom door but no-one can remember when it was last used. It has become more a symbol of what might be the ultimate sanction. Not even much of a warning if the dust collecting on it is anything to go by. But they are surprised that no punishment seems to be forthcoming. Quite the opposite. They would all like to have taken a gentle stroll up Church Field.

Instead it is Isaac Pawsey for all his failings who has this privilege. He doesn't understand it either but, grateful for the chance to redeem himself, off he goes.

Half an hour later he is back. The character with him is hard to fathom. He is certainly not old but appears stooped and weather-worn. His clothes were once fine but that was probably when they were the property of someone else. There are a couple of small dogs at his feet. In many ways, they look better nourished and better cared-for than he does. He clutches a bundle of papers as though they are his most precious possessions. And he smells. Even to boys from mean backgrounds, he does not smell good.

None of this is the fault of his 'landlord.' Unbeknown to the class, the schoolmaster has been speaking to Candler Bird. Past differences have for the time being been put to one side. Mr. Bird has encountered none other than Jemmy Chambers, a wandering poet. Prompted more by the expectations of his elevated status than any real compassion, he has offered a straw-covered corner in his barn and the promise of a bath. Unfortunately the second offer has been declined. Others have tried to 'help' Mr. Chambers, even offering him a cottage to live in but that is not his way. Whether his choice of resting place is more to do with what he sees as the requirements for his creativity or a natural inclination towards a nomadic way of life it is hard to say. It is easier to understand the man through his verse than what he has to say about himself.

It seems a good idea to decamp to the churchyard, where Mr. Chambers is persuaded to read from his works to the boys, his small dogs nestled by his feet.

> "By yonder bridge and straddling rippling stream
> I knew the softening sun, sustaining, warm:
> I stood with eyes soft-blear'd as in a dream,
> And saw the harshest peltings of a wint'ry storm.
> I knew the worst that Heaven had to fling,
> And tho' t'was nature's choice alone that time
> To favour me with God's gifts beckoning,
> My comfort brief, but comfort so sublime.

Much of his work proves to be equally bleak, but there are lighter moments in his verses: poems on the subjects of fairs, the roads he has travelled and the kindness he has met along the way. The boys are intrigued by a rhyme that tells of a rat that destroyed a length of twine.

> "In minutes nocturnal," said I, "while in bed
> The rat was destroying and spoiling my thread.
> Behold this new twine, once substantial and strong
> 'Tis gnawed into pieces but three inches long."

Thomas Warren is not sure what he wants the boys to learn from this, but it is a pleasant break from their normal curriculum and one they will not forget in a hurry. It is timely that he has thought to do this as Jemmy Chambers, itinerant poet, will soon take himself off and, together with his dogs, will be residing in somebody else's barn or outhouse and having his doggerel read and proclaimed to be great poetry in some other corner of Suffolk. They know this because Isaac Pawsey goes in search of him two days later to read him a few lines he has composed himself. But the space in the barn is empty. The man and his dogs and his poems have gone.

Though she has not visited the school for some time, Martha Palmer is back. For an illicit relationship to flourish requires two things - opportunity and intent. Briefly both were there and it is possible that the master and his comely assistant have seen fit at least to remove the opportunity for a while. Not that there are many opportunities. Eight lively schoolboys and a growing family are putting paid to that. Now she has returned, and such feelings as can exist between them must gently simmer for the time being. Thomas is a realist. There cannot be any future to it. He is only too aware that he belongs to an earlier generation than Martha and surely she must be bound to find a lad of her own age, mustn't she?

The Warrens are 'trying for another baby.' That is Beth's decision rather than his and 'trying' is about as far as it has got so far. Nights can be cold at that end of the Guildhall. Often the whole family finds itself bedded together for warmth. As autumn nudges summer out of the way, the first frosts warn them of what is to come.

What is to come is a winter to be reckoned with. They have long cold winters often enough. This will be longer and colder than anyone can remember. When snow first falls, as early as the last week in November, it becomes commonplace for boys unable to make the journey home to bed down on the floor in front of the dying embers of the fire. It is far too early to plunder too much of their precious wood-store.

But learning must go on. The boys are grasping more than just the the fundamentals of mathematics. With the help of a home-made abacus all should soon be able to handle numbers up to and beyond a thousand. Some of their fathers may still need a tally-stick to keep check of sacks of grain on the farms where they work, but Thomas Warren has higher aspirations for their sons. They can use Imperial measures and, more to the point, recognise when a marketeer or tradesman is attempting to supply them with under-length cloth or underweight meat. And should they ever be called upon to keep a table of accounts, these boys, better than most passing through his charge, will be perfectly capable too of managing that.

It is after the first fall of snow has withered away and a biting wind hurries over the hill from the west that he shoos the boys outside for a while to burn off a little energy. There is nothing worse than trying to teach a class that has been shut up inside for too long. Everyone becomes restless; the master included. So the door is flung open wide and all eight exit noisily into the nearby churchyard where they are unlikely to disturb its more ancient inhabitants... The only other living occupant at that moment being Old Southgate employed in the annual task of laying more gravel on the church path.

The one thing to be said about the clothes supplied by the Trustees is that they are warm and hard-wearing. Those like John Coats and Tom Brett whose growth upwards has been slow have not needed to have their jackets altered or replaced. The bigger lads like George Buckle, Sam Tricker and Henry Robinson are on their second set. Charging around the churchyard like frantic hares on heat, they seem to be able to brave the coldest of the weather.

The master is preparing for a lesson in writing when Jerry Sharman bursts in. Thick hair, wind-tossed and all over the place, he seems to have lost his cap. Thomas Warren is about to ask where he has put it (none of the the boys is supposed to be seen out unless wearing the complete set of clothes supplied). Before the missing item has time to be mentioned, Jerry has news to share.

"Please Mr. Warren, there's a whully odd ol' man outside," he says, breathlessly.

They both step out to see that what Jerry describes is not far short of the fact. Another of the boys hands Jerry his cap. They have been playing some kind of game of 'catch' with it. Now the game has been abandoned in favour of the latest distraction. The man he describes is indeed 'whully odd.' He is short, little taller than most of the boys, and corpulent with a ruddy complexion. He is well-dressed but seems somewhat confused both as to where he is and, more to the point, where he is supposed to be. He has on a brown coat, red patterned waistcoat, a new hat and a full-bottomed wig. He has a broad but confused grin across his face.

"We asked him his name but all he say is 'six-and-ninepence', reports Sam Tricker.

And for good measure, that is exactly what the man says. Some of the boys laugh and the man responds by smiling, removing his hat and bowing as if used to being a source of other people's amusement.

Never having met the man before, it is hard to be sure whether he is disordered in his mind or just playing the fool. Fortunately, it will not be long before the question is answered for them. Coming along the road on horseback are two concerned riders, a man and a woman. They are calling out as they look from side to side. And the words they are calling sound suspiciously like, "six and ninepence." Hearing their call, the 'whully odd' visitor lifts his head and echoes their words.

It transpires that nearby Waltham Hall has a new tenant, Mr. Williams. He has been attempting to move his whole household from Essex. The change has proved confusing to one of them. The unfortunate gentleman who has found his way to Earl Stonham churchyard has indeed a disorder of the brain. Mr. Williams explains: “I found him being offered for sale on Harwich Quayside. They had dressed him in girl’s clothing and were making him dance for the people’s amusement. I couldn’t bear to see any human being treated like that so I bid for him, and I think you can guess how much I ended up paying for him.”

“Was it six and ninepence, sir?” asks Samuel Tricker.

“Indeed it was,” replies Mr. Williams. He works in our household, though to be honest I think we look after him rather more than the other way about. He finds change hard to adjust to, and our move to Stonham Parva, I am afraid, has confused him even more than usual. Still we are very grateful you have found him and looked after him in our absence. You must accept a reward. The visitor then holds out a coin the like of which few sitting there have seen before - worth rather more than the six and ninepence that has been spoken of - a guinea. It shines bright and unblemished as only gold can, the royal shield of George III showing it for what it is. Mr. Warren is all for refusing the gift, but Mr. Williams is insistent, pressing the coin into his hand and folding his fingers over it.

“Then we thank you sir,” says the master, “and be assured it will be used to the boys’ advantage.”

Then they all watch from the churchyard as the three walk their horses back in the direction of Waltham Hall. After which, James Nunn asks if a small piece of paper might be forthcoming and, to the delight of the rest of the class, with quill and ink produces a sketch of no small talent of the man they now remember as ‘six and ninepence.’ They find a pin and hang it in pride of place on the classroom wall. There it will hang until rust from the pin discolours the paper and the ink begins to fade.

Regarding the guinea, Thomas Warren is as good as his word. He promised the gift would be used to advance the boys’ education. As it will. A month later after a visit to a St. Edmundsbury shop, good sturdy books (not new, but good and sturdy) will be purchased. And the class of ’63, now the class of ’64 will be the first of many to benefit from the gift.

Chapter 7 ~ December 1764

Then there is a mild spell. It starts to rain on the Friday afternoon and keeps on well into Sunday evening. The fields are running with water and the old Guildhall isn't a lot better. A lot of the labourers are only employed on casual contracts and have been laid off. Those hired for the year have been hedging and clearing ditches and gulleys. It is as well they have, but it isn't enough. Not when it is like this. Once in a while it rains as if Noah might still be around. This is one of those times. The streams and rivers are full to overflowing and there is more to come. Down in the bottom of the valley, Thomas Warren can sense how vulnerable they are.

Already you can't reach the Scole Road or Stonham Aspal. The Lady Bridge across to Creeting is lost under a torrent. The hill rising up to Forward Green is like a waterfall, and the track up the hill to the rectory has great ruts running with muddy water. All traffic has ceased. Even if an intrepid child should stagger along muddy paths to school, it is unlikely there will be much done by way of education this week.

Even when the rain stops, the river goes on rising. And then it starts all over again. Just as it seems they will be awash, the current swirling inches below the doorstep, the sun comes out and the sky clears. But this is December. The temperature plummets and ice fringes the flooded valley. Icicles grow from the eaves to the ground. The winter has become relentless. For two months, everything that nature has in its arsenal is unleashed upon Thomas Warren and his beleaguered family. Lessons are spasmodic affairs delivered to a few boys at a time. John Coats and Sam Tricker are not seen for weeks, and that is hardly a surprise. To make the journey once in a day would be like an expedition into an Arctic wasteland. Twice would be unthinkable.

Slowly the flood level drops and portions of the road become visible again. But then there is snow to contend with, and after that the thaw. One day in early February when melting snow has raised the river level again, concerned for those living down there, a boat is sculled up to their door from the tap-room by the crossroads. Someone has brought supplies. A kind thought, and necessary too with two hungry children to be fed. It is the time of year when food is never plentiful. Meat from the cull of livestock at the end of the summer has run low, hens are off the lay, fish is hard to obtain with transport so affected and supplies of potatoes, beans and wheat exhausted. It is never hard to fast for Lent. The winter has already seen to that, especially this year.

Then all at once, it is over. The world is an altogether better place and things, if not exactly back to normal, are heading in the right direction. First there is the clearing up. You can hardly tell where the road used to run, so much debris fills the space. Earth and stones, some large enough to designate boulders, branches, even whole trees, half a plough and the carcass of a sheep.

John Coats Senior, in his capacity as an overseer, pays a visit to assess the damage to the Guildhall. Shovelled banks of earth have kept the flood at bay at ground level, but so much water has percolated through roof and walls that a permanent smell of mould pervades the place. What is more, you can hear the rats in the thatch.

"I would say this building is past repairing," Mr. Coats says, "but it is unlikely I'll be listened to." He itemises the numerous faults with the Guildhall. So many times, all this has been committed to paper and that has been an end to it. Once again Thomas Warren is left to anticipate a further period of patch-up and mend, after which the school will be designated 'sound' (until the next time).

Now there will be a certain urgency. Warmer, longer days will mean demands will be made on the boys from all sides. At home there will be a host of jobs for them to do. At school there will be an attempt to make up for lost time or at least to restore their skills to what they had been months before. Six of them have to be prepared for their confirmation, and only a few weeks to do it.

Two of the lads, George Buckle and Henry Robinson have been with the schoolmaster for three years and will now come to terms with the prospect of an apprenticeship. The elders of the parish have been negotiating on their behalf. It is a way they can see of breaking the cycle of dependency that has come about in certain families over generations. Poor beget poor and so it goes on. Consulting the Overseers' books of payments made to the needy of the parish reveals decades of the same names in receipt of parish relief. Taking a boy from that background and preparing him for a trade may mean his name will not feature alongside that of his parents and grandparents.

The two school-leavers seem all at once so young, but for Henry it won't be too much of a wrench. Ever the farm labourer's son, he will train in animal husbandry just a couple of villages away. George however is to venture much further. He will go to London and become a waterman on the Thames. And it doesn't seem to trouble him one bit. Excitedly he will bring in his apprenticeship indenture. He can't wait. The parish will pay for him to learn about tides and currents; even to read from maps and charts. They don't expect to see him back. And as far as he is concerned, London may be just the beginning of his travels. George is the one who has scanned the Ipswich Journal for tales of Lisbon and Genoa, Petersburg and Stockholm. Ever the adventurer, this indenture is significant in that it is his first move away from the only place the Buckle family has ever known. In their eyes he might be going to the other side of the world. As far as George sees it, this is just the first step of many.

Two down: that leaves six boys who may or may not choose to stay at the school for a final year. After which the class of '63 will be scattered and, hopefully helped to make more of themselves. For that, Thomas Warren knows better than most, is what all this is about.

Chapter 8 ~ Spring 1765

Spring has come in early March like a blessing on those who have held their faith. It may still be early to discount winter entirely, but as far as nature is concerned, those early balmy days are all the hint she needs to throw off the blanket of despair and begin to flourish. Not yet white with blossom, nor green with leaf, the blackthorn buds are just opening, giving a hint of both. Aconites are yellowing the banks, and ducks along the river and pheasants in the fields are paired, not flocked. Rooks are noisily snapping off twigs to repair what the winter's worst has made of their nests, and the early nesters - blackbird and dunnock, pigeon and pudneypoke - are already selecting sites with care, in anticipation of a bit of protection from promised leaf cover.

Old Southgate is back to gravel the churchyard paths once again - it must be Spring. Boys arrive noisily to school and Martha Palmer too makes a reappearance. She brings with her an amusing letter from an earlier copy of the Ipswich Journal. It may be amusing to some but all it does is make the master angry.

"The vanity and ambition of parents in educating their children above their proper stations in life..." he reads aloud, "...are such indulgencies as expose numbers continually to disappointment, misery and ruin."

'Who writes this stuff?' he wonders. Then Martha, eyes sparkling, directs his attention to lines penned further down the letter which read, "My object at present is the ill education that in general is given to daughters; which is always ill when not suitable to the sphere of life in which they were born."

It goes on at length, prompting Thomas Warren to feel like either tearing up the paper in disgust or alternatively, writing a reply. In the end he does neither and joins the others in laughing it off. At least in Earl Stonham the poor have a chance at a basic education, albeit only boys.

"You know what," he tells the class, "there will be a day when all children, and I don't only mean boys, will receive an education, in spite of what this fool maintains."

"What, even girls, sir?" asks Henry Robinson.

"And why would you see fit to object to that, Henry? Miss Palmer here has been educated to a level well beyond your present capabilities. I don't see that she or the rest of you have suffered from her expertise." And giving her a grin, he turns his attention back to the matter in hand, the questions and answers of the Catechism. Everybody's favourite!

It is Friday, later the same week, somewhere in the region of seven o'clock in the morning, and some fool is ringing the church bell as if their life depends upon it.

Beth Warren has turned over, unable or unwilling to acknowledge the interruption to her sleep. Thomas Junior is at the door. His father tries to grab a moment's peace.

"I know, I know. I have no idea what it is all about. Why don't you put a coat on and go and find out." 'After all,' he thinks, 'what are children for?'

In a very few minutes, the boy is back. "Mr. Garnham says the King has recovered from his sickness."

"Nobody here even knew he was sick," says his father, thinking to himself, '...nor cares much.' Clearly Mr. Garnham does care as he continues tolling the bell for some time. Eventually, Candler Bird arrives and suggests he might like to give it a rest.

"The trouble is, now the Norwich Machine passes the Brewery tap three times a week, people get to read the London papers and know the King's business almost as soon as His Majesty does." Candler Bird is as much of a royalist as the next man but can live without such blatant displays of regal loyalty.

Other people have begun to arrive to find out what it means. "Are we at war?" someone asks. Well, we usually are, but bells are rarely rung to publicise it. "Are we all supposed to gather here?" asks another. For some it is a good excuse to delay getting to work. Others are genuinely troubled. Ironically, it will prove to be Mr. Garham's last contribution to village life. It has all been too much for his enfeebled frame. Within weeks, his body will lie close to the tower where he so recently had disturbed the village with his ringing. His 'estate' will be advertised for sale and his belongings auctioned off. 'Estate' is how it will be described in the Ipswich Journal, but really it is a modest farmhouse with tumble-down outbuildings and just forty acres of land. Thomas Warren will buy the dead man's chickens and be responsible for continual complaints from the parishioners every time they encounter them foraging amongst the graves in the churchyard.

A schoolmaster expects to be surprised once in a while by the children in his charge. But it is a surprise when it happens. The Sharman boy is a case in question. He has a rare fascination - a talent for numbers. He has been watching his father sowing seed. In February, it was barley seed broadcast onto frosty ground. More recently, it has been carrot seed. It is a skilled job to spread the seed evenly and waste little, but Jerry Sharman is sure it could be done with more efficiency. Even a skilled sower will never plant a field evenly enough to allow for differences in fertility of the land. If immediately harrowed in, much still ends up on the surface and feeds the pigeons. John Coats has found out the weight of barley seed required to plant an acre of land and Jerry has calculated that fine furrows on well-harrowed soil would produce a more even crop if a way could be found to sow the seed in lines. He can even tell you what the savings might be. That is what his teacher finds remarkable. Now he has Sam Tricker interested and the pair of them spend hours poring over figures. James Nunn is called in to design such a tool.

"The way I see it," says Jerry, you need to open a furrow, drop in the seed and rake it over again, so 't'int one tool, it's three." Naturally, George Buckle appoints himself arbiter of their ideas.

"That 'un't work," he says helpfully.

Others in the class mock them lightly, Tom Brett especially. "Thass jus' theery - in't real farmin'," he chaffs, whilst secretly admiring their diligence and perseverance.

Thomas Warren doen't like to tell them that such a machine has already been invented even if nobody round there seems to put their faith in it.

Even now the winter is over, food is scarce and expensive. Corn especially is a case in question. Everyone needs corn for his daily bread, but who can afford it as prices spiral ever higher? Dunnington and Cook, the local millers are complaining because no-one is bringing corn to be ground. They want to know if it is being hand-querned like in the old times. But they know the truth of the matter is that a few people with corn to spare are holding onto it, waiting for the price to rise still further. The shortage is causing anger among those who find that something as simple as the price of a loaf of bread is outside their earning capacity. They grind whatever seed comes their way but it is poor stuff with little or no sustenance. Children are coming to school hungry. Hunger makes them all irritable. And the master finds the boys are more inattentive than usual. This group of eight has been his class for over eighteen months and he wonders if they aren't all a little over-familiar with one another, but really it is down to malnutrition as are so many of the problems that emerge at this time of year.

Sam Tricker is upset. He will only attend for half a day for, as his mother explains, "His uncle Ben died the other day. We need to get to the funeral." Inattention killed him. The Coroner says the three pints of ale didn't help, but somehow he came off the waggon he was driving and ended up under the wheels. It's a common enough story. No food, just enough alcohol to convince your body you're not starving, a bump in the road, and that's that! The Coroner says he shouldn't have been sitting on the shafts, but if you're going to put a decent load aboard, there's not really anywhere else to sit. So that afternoon, the class is reduced by one.

The following day, it is Isaac Pawsey who is missing.

"He cut his hand picking stones from our fields," explains John Coats. "It is very sore. He keeps crying." Later they hear he is sick with fever and the hand is showing signs of a mortification of the wound. Eventually, the Overseers see fit to paying Dr. Cooper, a surgeon from Mendlesham, to treat the boy. He lets a little blood, leaves a powder and departs a guinea the richer. Though there are those that doubt the likely efficacy of this treatment, within days the wound is healing. His aunt puts it down to her own comfrey poultice.

Things go in threes. That is what they all say. Thomas Warren's mother used to assert this, and his wife now says the same. So, when James Nunn falls ill they all say it was bound to happen. A sensitive boy, James has shown a talent for drawing. He makes sketches on any surface available, using the simplest of materials - chalk, charcoal, home-made colours applied with quills, reed-pens and makeshift brushes. Occasionally, the master gives him a piece of paper in the hope he will be encouraged to make the most of such an opportunity. Where the plaster on one wall of the schoolroom has flaked alarmingly during the winter, Mr. Warren has smoothed it and, knowing it will soon be limewashed, has offered it to the boy for his very own mural. He has decided it will be a picture of the boys and their master.

What has barely been started remains the way it was when he was last at school. It is uncertain when it will next be attended to. Henry Robinson has spoken to James' mother, but is not to be allowed anywhere near the boy himself. Even his own father is to stay away for fear he will transmit the disease to his fellow workers and their families. For it is feared James Nunn has diphtheria. He has a high temperature and a swollen neck. He complains of a sore throat. So far, other confirming symptoms have not been observed, but the family are taking every precaution possible.

"He can't breathe proper and he can't swaller," explains Henry. It is not a good month. One thing after another. The parish has good reason to fear diphtheria. An outbreak five years earlier took the lives of a handful of children including Thomas Brett's baby sister.

But James Nunn, like Isaac Pawsey, is made of stronger stuff and, whatever it was that laid him low for a while, soon he is back to make his presence felt and to finish his mural. Remarkable likenesses of the eight boys and Mr. Warren their master will decorate the room until one morning they arrive at school to discover that James Nunn's act of creativity has been turned back to a plain white wall. Even Mr. Warren says it is a bit of a shame really.

Chapter 9 ~ Early Summer 1765

A small group, through the act of being together over time, moulds itself into a unit. The class of '63, now the class of '65 has been unchanged throughout that time. Soon two of them will go their separate ways, leaving the parents of those that remain to decide whether their sons are to 'wear the clothes' for another year. But it may not prove that simple. It **will** not prove that simple! Although these periods of learning together have generated a special comradeship, still it won't take much to undo it, unravel it, unpick it and unfasten it.

Farmers in the district around Earl Stonham employ only so many men and boys as they can gainfully occupy during the lean months of winter. These may be permanent labourers or those hired for a year at a time, usually at the Michaelmas hirings. In the busier times of late spring and especially during harvest when more hands are needed, others will be taken on temporarily or paid just an hourly rate.

So lesser hirings are organised where farmers can assess the relative physical prowess of the men in front of them. It is May and a number seeking employment have gathered at the Pye Inn along the turnpike at Stonham Parva. A certain amount of drink is available. Farmers can assess in this way how wedded some of them are to the local ale. On the other hand, there are those farmers who will use it to their advantage, contracting a man at a lower rate on account of his inability to notice what he is signing.

John Coats Senior is looking for another man. He is prepared to pay slightly above the common rate for the right candidate. He needs someone strong and committed; experienced with the variety of animals found on a mixed farm. He needs a man with his own tools for hoeing, reaping and threshing and the ability to use them for long hours without much respite. The man should be sober and trustworthy, and a good communicant member of the Church of England, of course.

He thinks he has found the man he needs. Thomas Sharman certainly looks the part. He is tall and, though well into his forties, looks fitter and stronger than many of the younger men offering their services. It seems surprising in a way that he is not already contracted. He has worked with horses and looked after sheep and dairy cattle.

"You are available to begin at once?" asks Coats.

"I am, sir," answers Sharman.

John Coats casts a glance at the others waiting hopefully to attract his attention. He is tempted to enquire further about one or two of them, but he knows he may lose the services of this man if he does so. He makes the decision.

"You would be prepared to sign to work for me till Michaelmas, after which we may make it a more permanent arrangement?" He knows he has one man working for him whose age may well see him discharged after this Summer.

"Indeed I would, sir."

"And you are a member of our church? It is just... I don't recall seeing you there much."

"My wife, Elizabeth takes the children every Sunday. I have been preferring to attend in Mendlesham, the village where where I was baptised. My boy has been studying at the school with your son, if you remember. We help to keep the churchyard tidy." All the right answers - so it seems.

Then, just as quill and ink are produced, the next man in the line steps forward. He looks rather older by comparison, though he is actually only five years senior. He is shorter, not much above five foot four, but rugged; typical build for a Suffolk labourer.

"I think there is something you oughter know, Mr. Coats, sir. When he say he go to church in Mendlesham, I think you might ask him where exactly that might be. It in't just Church of England you find along that road - them what gets called Quakers go that way too!"

For whilst a man may happily hold on to such dangerous knowledge as will deprive another of his livelihood for as long as it has no effect on him, once it becomes a matter of feeding his own family, the secret soon becomes a secret no longer.

"Just you ask him where it is he might be goin' when he walk past my house three times a week."

It is hard to ascertain what Thomas Sharman's thoughts on the matter are. There are no threats, no punches thrown, not even so much as a glare of contempt. Two years of communing with the Brotherhood have ensured that. When it becomes clear that Mr. Coats is unlikely to be employing him now, he moves away in search of an employer whose priorities may be different.

And as he had hoped, it is Thomas Brett senior who will benefit from this unfortunate act of revelation. But it will have another rather more profound effect. Jerry Sharman will not be returning to the school after the harvest is gathered in. Mr. Coats will have spoken to the Trustees on the matter and this is another from the class of '63 who will be expected to freshly make his way in the world. He will see the school year out, but after that, taking what he has learned, he will venture on.

Fortunately, Candler Bird takes a more enlightened attitude regarding his employment of Elizabeth Sharman. As far as he is concerned, all such affairs lie in the hands of Mrs. Bugg, the housekeeper. Washing his own hands of the matter, he leaves the decision to her. In such ways, uncomfortable decisions can be handled with a minimum of disturbance and disruption.

Candler Bird has an idea. Thomas Warren has again been complaining that his stipend is pathetically poor. And of course, he is right. But for reasons formerly explained it is not likely to improve in a hurry. So, ever-imaginative, Mr. Bird has come up with an answer.

"We have a few things that need doing," he explains. In other words, all the paperwork that no-one in the parish wants to do needs to be completed by someone vaguely literate. This is not the way Candler explains it. He is far more tactful than that. The outcome is that Thomas Warren will write letters and terriers on behalf of the churchwardens and overseers in return for certain payments that may or may not be entered up into the accounts in that manner.

The Accounts of Mr. Candler Bird
Churchwarden.

In a way, Candler Bird is being at his most creative. To be honest, he quite likes the deskwork, but it is becoming difficult to find time for it. He is never so happy as when writing a sheet of parish accounts or drafting a letter in his capacity as churchwarden. He loves filling a page with finely crafted ink. You can tell from the way his exquisite hand-writing is illuminated with faces set into the circular letters, and curls and squirls attach themselves elegantly to the text. So, in truth he is making a small sacrifice.

"Also," he adds, "I have a task for you this summer." What this amounts to is teaching some of his children to swim.

"I am nearly sixty years old," he explains. "Being a father to tiny children at my age is not easy, I can tell you. Good heavens, they expect me to chase them and climb trees and tell them stories. If I didn't employ a nursemaid, I wouldn't get a moment's peace. I have seven children and now my good lady tells me she's with child again! We love living at Deerbolts, but we have a problem. Mary is terrified our children are all going to drown in the lake. The little devils are fascinated by water - won't stay away from it."

Candler explains that he remembers from somewhere that Thomas Warren can swim. "So as you teach, and you can swim, maybe I could pay you to teach my little tribe to swim. That way, they are happy, the wife is happy and you and I are happy. Now Thomas, how about it?"

Then as Warren pauses, he adds, "I am right - you can swim can't you?"

"Yes, sorry, I was thinking of years ago when it was hot and we'd dip in the river below the Botanic Gardens in Bury. And if it was really nice, they'd run waggons out to Ampton and Livermere. That was where my father taught me to swim. And of course, in the winter when everything froze, we'd go out there again to slide and skate and play games on the ice. It's funny, I hadn't thought of that for ages."

"So, I am right, you could teach my children to swim enough to be safe around the water?"

"You know what, I don't think I have swum for over ten years, but it's something you never forget. And I agree with you. They should be able to swim, or have enough fear of water to stay well away from it. I don't see why I can't wander up and over the hill a few times this Summer: but it will only be when it is warm enough. I may not be as old as you but even I don't relish shivering in freezing water. The water in your lake will not be that inviting for any of us unless accompanied by a good deal of sunshine overhead."

This is an admirable arrangement. Thomas Warren is so captivated by it, he has not even asked how much he is to receive in payment. Maybe he can even teach his own children to swim.

But first, there is a school year to complete. Educating eight boys - teaching them all that they might need to know whatever their future endeavours.

The time together is drawing to a close. Soon, some of the boys will be off and away to begin their adult lives though they are hardly adults in any sense of the word. This is the time when lighter moments creep into the classroom. As if even the master knows he can relax the normal discipline and enjoy what comes from it. One memorable moment comes after the class has been set a problem to solve together as a team. It is proving difficult.

"None onnus have gotta clue where to start," remarks George.

"Has," says the master.

"Wassat?"

"Has - None of us *has* got a clue."

"I don't unnerstan'" says George.

"None is singular - so it should be 'none of us has' - or, as you might put it, 'None onnus *has* gotta clue'." Thomas Warren mocks the boy's accent. The class laugh.

"Well," replies George, "That sound wrong when I say it like that. You sayin' it is different to how I do it."

"Different *from*," irritatingly remarks the master.

"Come agin."

"Different from: opposite to."

"Oh pardon me for speakin'," says George, sounding hurt. But you can never really put that boy down for long, and by now he knows to take it all in good grace and the humour with which it was intended to be received.

From time to time, the Trustees put in an appearance and the master is glad to demonstrate how well this group has learned under his guidance. Robert Plowman and the new curate, Sam Ringe arrive unannounced one morning and Warren takes the opportunity to explain how much better he could do his job if only a little more money was made available for the basic tools - paper and ink, for example. He knows, because he has looked at the Town Accounts, that fifteen shillings is regularly put aside for those very materials so the Parish Clerk can do his work. He is only asking for little more.

"I really do not understand why, when my boys have reached this level of proficiency, there is any argument regarding their right to use pen and paper."

What Thomas Warren also knows is the money allotted by the parish elders to what may loosely be described as entertainment. The account books reveal it. There is money enough to pay the ringers to chime in the New Year and serve them cakes and ale. The same is true at Christmas, and over £4 pays for the leading citizens to celebrate November 5th each year. There seems to be no shortage of money then, does there? But there is only so much that one such as he can offer by way of protest. And he has learnt over the last ten years who are the likely ones to be more responsive to his requests, and when and how to ask. This time there is a promise of more paper. He will have to keep on at them to ensure they keep their word.

Ironically they do have news of money to be spent. It is an idea borrowed from another charity school. On leaving, boys are to be presented with a Bible into which they will, in their neatest handwriting, enter a promise. This will say in so many words that should they ever aspire to owning the sum of fifty pounds or more, ten pounds will be donated to the Earl Stonham School fund. This is a promise unlikely to need remembering by many of its pupils. But Thomas Warren offers his gratitude for their consideration, as he continues to demonstrate what his pupils have achieved.

This is one of those days when Martha Palmer is there. If the Trustees are concerned about this working relationship, they say nothing. Martha is charming, as always, and they warm to her, thanking her for her efforts in the classroom.

But their stay is short. Other issues are on their minds. There has been much taking of game from copses and coverts in the parish and an advert has been placed in the Ipswich Journal warning those 'loose and idle fellows' responsible that they are likely to be prosecuted. It is all hot air. Everyone knows perfectly well who the local poachers are and they'll not be reading the paper. They may be skilled at laying a snare, but most have never learned to read a word. And the Constable, for his twenty-seven shillings a year is hardly likely to forsake his sleep and go chasing about in the darkness of the early morning.

The only one who might be concerned to read such an advertisement is Isaac Pawsey. He and his older brother John regularly accompany their father Jacob in pursuit of the food of the rich. Bread may come at a premium but the Pawsey family don't seem to lack nourishment. In place of corn and bread and cereal, they dine on pheasant and hare and partridge. Many is the morning at this time of year when Isaac Pawsey will be found dozing on his desk. But Thomas Warren cannot complain. Once in a while, a small gift will find its way into his kitchen, as like as not.

John Coats has brought a gift too. This time it is for the whole class. His family have been to Ipswich Races. There has been far more than racing to see - a fair and a market offering sweets and confectionery, examples of which are shared around.

"The King gave a prize in one race of one hundred guineas," he tells the class, though no-one can possibly imagine how much that is worth. "They had cock-fighting," he continues, "and actors in tents acting plays." As a child, he had been barred from experiencing the blood and gore of a main of cocks, but other entertainments had been more acceptable to the sensibilities of the young.

What he does not tell them is one aspect of the trip that has continued to disturb him. A man from nearby Kesgrave has died. What he is not sure is exactly how. But everyone seems very angry about it. They say he has killed himself, but John thinks this cannot be right. Surely that is not possible. You have to live until God decides it is time for you to die like Thomas Brett's little sister a few years ago. John Coats in his innocence cannot imagine such a thing as suicide. They have been saying at the race track that the man's body has been taken to the crossroads and buried - not in the churchyard, but in a place where people and animals may trample over his remains. But what is worse, a stake has been driven through his heart before he has been covered up. That is what one of the showman's sons has told him at the races. It seems all too terrible and certainly is not something he would wish to share with his friends. But he can't forget it and, true or not, it dwells on his mind, so he can be found at odd moments with a dark expression on his face or a tear of fear on his cheek.

Then, something else, almost as dark. In church, on Sunday, the boys attend wearing 'the clothes.' The mothers find this inconvenient. When are they supposed to be washed and dried? But of course, Sunday is not meant to be a day of such labour, and besides, the Trustees expect their call for attendance to be observed. The new curate, Reverend Ringe reads out what he calls 'letters patent'. They are pieces of information needing publication, and where better than from the pulpit? Often these involve new laws and the promised punishments facing offenders. Also they include briefs announcing collections for those unfortunate enough to be suffering fire, disease, or loss of some kind. They are unknown names, often far away in unknown places, for whom it is hard to feel any great depth of sympathy. Where exactly is Devon or Lancaster or Durham? But there will be a house-to-house collection nevertheless, and those who can spare a shilling, a penny, or the widow's mite will contribute towards a small parish donation. Though it may be small, combined with other equally small amounts from other parishes, a significant sum will finally make its way to the beneficiary, in an attempt to alleviate one tiny pocket of misery in this world.

This week, the sufferers are not that far away. In Wattisham in Suffolk lives a family by the name of Downing who have been miserably afflicted by an unknown and terrifying ailment that has killed one child and maimed the rest of the family. Some horrific unknown disease has cast its shadow over the Downing family for three years now. Their limbs have rotted and, like a leprosy, one by unfortunate one, taken from them their useful lives. You can't help but be glad it is not your own family, and this time the people of Earl Stonham will be most generous. As will others. They will respond, not just because the appeals have been most graphic in nature. But because there but for God's grace it might be happening to any of them.

And what will it buy Mr. Downing and his family? A slightly more comfortable last few years in spite of all their disabilities. A rather grander monument than they had any right to expect in Wattisham church. The last resting place of what remains of their embattled bodies.

The Journal will list the names of the greatest givers, neglecting to recognise the pennies from the poor. A little more for them to feel bitter about. Never mind: their time is soon to come.

Chapter 10 -~ August 1765

Then the world falls in. That is how it seems for a time, when everything comfortable and familiar becomes turned upside down. There are those still living who remember being told by their grandparents of a time when it was very much like that - when father was pitched against son; brother against brother in support of King or Parliament. But all that is long gone and no-one had thought such times could ever return. Now they are beginning to think again.

Thomas Warren has never really regarded himself as belonging to the labouring classes. He may be paid as poorly as many of them but he has some kind of status in the community. Churchwardens and Overseers tilt their hat to him in passing. He is educated, literate, respected. But his sympathies... now that is a different matter. If it ever comes to manning or dismantling barricades, he knows only too well whose side he will be on. Even though he is not a violent man, he would, he thinks, be prepared to defend what is right.

Which is why he finds himself in a dilemma, not of his own design. It is early August, warm, and the corn stands golden in the summer sun. But in spite of it all, prices are still high. The Cook family, millers across the turnpike in Stonham Aspal have been grinding corn for generations. Their mill is rarely still. Their mill-stones are sharpened more regularly than most and they are renowned for the quality of their flour. But now word is passed around that they are in league with local farmers to keep the price artificially high. As are other millers in the district. Under the summer's heat, discontent festers. At first it is just clusters of men with nothing better to do with their time than assembling and mouthing accusations. Most men, after all, are involved in the harvest. But empty stomachs and only small beer to fill them is scant reward for long days in the fields. Soon there is talk of pulling down windmills, burning bakeries and plundering barns. It may not be revolution - not yet - but it has unnerved those with the most to lose.

Candler Bird arrives with William Scapy for support. They have a proposition for the schoolmaster now that he has no class to teach for a while. Typically, they assume he is better informed than he is.

"You know what is happening over at Bulchamp and Nacton of course?"

There is no 'of course' about it. He has not an inkling of what they are talking about.

"I am sorry gentlemen, but down here we are a little out on a limb you know."

"Surely you have been following matters in the Journal?"

Thomas Warren's blank look tells them all they need to know. He needs it all explaining.

Too many parishes are finding they are peopled by miscreants and malcontents," says Scapy. "So far, we have escaped much of it, but the time will come when we shall need to be ready for the worst."

Candler Bird at last realises the master needs a more thorough explanation as to their visit.

"Managing the needs and demands of our poor has quite rightly been our own responsibility for the last century or two. In Earl Stonham, we have had our share of problem families, but we have coped efficiently, frugally but fairly." He draws a long breath before continuing. "Other parishes have found value in combining together in unions to deal with the problem on a larger scale. We have our own Town Houses, furnished by the parish, simply but adequately and till now that has sufficed. Where people can do a little work, they are encouraged to do so, though most are elderly or infirm. However, it seems the time has come to follow the lead of others and build a Union House for the Bosmere Hundred to which thirty-four parishes have agreed to contribute. A site at Barham has been surveyed and building will commence as soon as the present disturbances die down."

"I still don't understand what this has to do with me," says Warren.

"If you had been reading your newspapers," reprimands Scapy, you would already know the trouble this is causing. In addition to the corn price problem and the Summer heat, people have been provoked to riot and disorder. At Nacton as fast as they try to build, the beggars pull it down again. The Blything House of Industry was virtually built and the mob destroyed it. The Military have had to be brought in to restore order."

"The thing is," says Candler Bird, "all available Parish Constables are being drafted to Barham to protect the builders, which leaves us wide open. It only needs a few hotheads to storm Dunnington's mill or set fire to tinder-dry fields and we could have a major insurrection on our hands."

"In Earl Stonham?" Thomas Warren can hardly believe what he is hearing.

"Very much in Earl Stonham," says Scapy, "so we are in need of a civic-minded fellow with the time to spare to deputise as Constable for the time being - make sure the feckless few don't give us a Summer to remember for all the wrong reasons!"

"I'll give it some thought," says Warren, hoping they will just go away and forget all about it.

"You'll do more than that if I have any say in the matter."

"Excuse me, Mr. Scapy," he says, "but I thought this was a voluntary position."

"When I was in the army and they asked for volunteers, you didn't ignore the request. Not if you had any real sense of responsibility"

Thomas Warren is becoming increasingly irritated by the man most of the villagers call 'Scabby.' So, he sidles up to Candler Bird. "Look, Can; I'll be beside your lake this afternoon. We'll talk about it then, alright?"

This may or may not have been enough to satisfy the 'military man', but it becomes clear to all present that no further decisions will be made just then, and the meeting breaks up.

Several times that summer, Warren has tried to tempt his son to join him in learning to swim in the Deerbolts Hall lake, but as in most interactions with his father, he chooses not to comply, preferring the company of his mother. So it will be just the school-master who will ascend the hill to meet Candler Bird later that afternoon.

Under the shade of alders and willows at the side of the mere, the subject is broached again.

"Look, I don't want to be awkward, but I find that man brings out the worst in me. If I had to break up a fracas between he and some of his workers, it would not be hard to side with the men. Was he really in the army? I've not heard about it."

"Actually, I think he was a minor officer in the Militia, but let's not dwell on that. The truth is he is right about one thing. We are due some trouble, and at least you might be able to talk some sense into the outragers before it comes to the sorry state of affairs they've had in Dorset." He uses the word 'outragers', which has Warren wondering if such a word exists, but whilst he might correct the English of his pupils, he knows when to leave well alone.

He has no idea what the problems have been in Dorset but he lets it pass. "You really think it might come to a confrontation?" he asks.

"Well they've arrested three dozen rioters from Nacton and as many at Halesworth. The gaols are full to bursting and

Dragoons are being sent from Bury to keep order there. I'm really not joking when I say we need you Thomas. I can't offer more than basic expenses and a staff of office. Not a lot to protect yourself with if the mob decide they don't like you. But please give it your serious thought."

After that, the rest of the afternoon is given over to demonstrating to the Bird children how they might avoid drowning. This time five of them have come down to the water's edge, encouraged by the heat. Warren has devised a harness attached to a rope and, one by one, he holds them up as they attempt to propel themselves through the icy-cold water in a variety of styles.

George is the first to really swim independently. The schoolmaster can sense when is the time to relax his hold on the rope and sure enough, the boy is really swimming. It will be a little while before he can be convinced that he genuinely is doing it all by himself. His two elder brothers, rather than be left behind by their small sibling, put all the more effort into their own swimming. The girls take a little longer, but the combination of good teaching and eighty-degree days will see all five looking fairly competent by the end of August.

Then with the new school term still three weeks away, Thomas Warren can hardly ignore the other demand that has been asked of him. So he takes the staff of a deputy and swears to uphold the laws of the land and of the parish, hoping against all hope he will not be expected to act in any capacity beyond the most basic.

The mill at Earl Stonham stands back from the road at Bells Cross, proudly, impressively. It is a relic of a past age, a post-mill of some antiquity. It is showing its age. It might last another generation, but its days are surely numbered. For all its failings, it is still a symbol of wealth and power. The miller and his family exude an air of affluence; they look well fed. For all that, the villagers don't envy the man or resent the fact that most of them will be in debt to him at some time in their lives. They know he works hard; as hard as any of them, and they know he is a craftsman, skilled at his craft. He has learned over the course of a lifetime how to get the most from his machinery. He does not cut corners. Already a pair of spare grindstones, newly-sharpened await hauling aloft to replace those worn flat from six months' friction. So, he is respected by all, and his comforts, such as they are, will not be resented too much by those he serves. At least, not usually; not in more moderate times. But these are not moderate times. Too many people are struggling to buy enough flour to bake a loaf of bread. Too many people are looking for someone to blame; someone to pour out their simmering discontent upon.

It is early evening and nearly a mile from the school, a crowd is gathering outside Earl Stonham mill. Mr. Dunnington has shut and bolted the doors and looks nervously from an upper window. He fears what may be coming. It has happened elsewhere and there is little he can do to prevent the mob storming his mill; threatening his livelihood. The local constables are no longer around to offer protection. All he can do is sit tight and hope.

"Mr. Warren, Mr. Warren, sir!"

There is a knocking at the Guildhall door to accompany the shouting. It is Henry Robinson. By chance, he is staying a few days at home with his parents.

"You gotta come, Mr. Warren, sir. There's trouble. A whole lot of men round the mill. They say they're goin' to wreck it."

There is no time to think further. Henry has run all the way, but it has taken him some time to get there and the mill could be in pieces already. So, grabbing his staff of office more as a potential weapon than a badge, Thomas Warren runs to 'borrow' a neighbour's pony. For some reason, it is saddled up ready for use by somebody. There is not time to ask, but needs must and, before many minutes have elapsed, he and Henry are sharing a ride up the hill to Forward Green. They are aware of smoke and flame but it is only down to someone having chosen to light the beacon. It's a long time since anyone has done that. The old way of calling people together. Master and pupil are relieved not to see further smoke on the horizon as they cross the green. Things haven't got that far yet. The pony struggles under their endeavours to hurry, but they do reach the scene in time. The confrontation developing at the front of the mill looks and sounds unpleasant, but that is all it is. A lot of yells and threats bordering on a riot, perhaps the onset of a skirmish, but not quite the full furore he had expected. Dismounting, he hands the reins to Henry, failing to notice the boy slip away in the opposite direction.

At the front of the crowd he recognises one or two of the men. Others among them are less familiar. Some are waving hats. There is a loud shouting of 'huzzas'. A few are clutching cudgels. He suspects they are agitators from elsewhere. He focuses his appeal on those he knows to be more reasonable.

"John Scotchmer, you must know this cannot be allowed to happen," he says in a reprimanding tone, well-rehearsed from the schoolroom. "And Philip Hicks. I understand your concerns but you can't threaten poor Mr. Dunnington. He is no more responsible for your plight than I am."

"Oh, we believe that all right. You'll be as bad as the rest on'em," says a foxy-faced man at the front. Warren has never seen him before and suspects he is one of a group believed to have stirred up trouble at Nacton.

"Excuse me," Warren says, lifting his staff of office to indicate his authority. "And just who might you be? You're not from round here. Why should Stonham people listen to you?"

Suddenly, at his shoulder, he is aware of Henry Robinson senior whispering into his ear. "My boy has gone for the military.

You try to keep 'em talking." Given the time to think, Thomas Warren might realise it will take at least an hour before he can expect relief. Instead, he looks around the crowd assembled. Some are from outside the village; they are the ones to be worried about. A few have already been swayed by what they have had to say. Most are just there because after a long day in the fields it is a relief to have an excuse not to work in their gardens. Some are genuinely angry; others just want to see what will happen next.

"Please, all of you. There is nothing to be gained from this."

"Oh no," says foxy-face, "You ask the miller where he keeps his store of best corn for grinding once the price gets too dear for any of us to afford."

"I feel very sorry for those who are suffering at this time," counters Warren, "but you don't seem poorly clad to me and I'll hazard a guess that you haven't had to walk all the way from Nacton or wherever you were last stirring up trouble."

Disturbingly, Warren sees one or two men are carrying switches that look and smell as though they have been soaked in pitch and rosin. This elevates matters to a whole new level. To fire a house would be illegal; even a capital offence: but to fire a mill could have consequences beyond imagining. Consequences for everyone standing there! The wooden building is tinder-dry and Warren knows only too well the explosive power of flour-dust. This is clearly less well understood by those clutching the tarred sticks. Their intention is only too clear, so desperately he calls to the men, "And what do you expect to do with them?"

"We don't need to supply answers to them as serves to protect the rich," shouts the man, and a few of the crowd echo their support. For all his words, it is hard to see what attracts the villagers to this less-than-pleasant character. The left side of his face is much pitted with black marks, the result of some past disease. He carries quite a paunch beneath his blue-lapelled coat with velvet collar and yellow metal buttons. This struggles to cover a spotted waistcoat, brown buckskin breeches and black ribbed stockings.

"This will achieve nothing," out-shouts Warren so the whole crowd can hear. They go quiet for a moment, and so he continues. "This man and his comrades have already been the cause of good men ending up in gaol. Thirty-five at Nacton alone! And isn't it remarkable, the ringleaders escaped. It isn't they who will spend the next months or years in prison regretting ever having anything to do with them. And those are the fortunate ones. Mark my words, this summer someone will end up on the end of a rope if this goes on. Or spending the rest of their lives picking tobacco in Virginia or Maryland. Now who is it to be? Not one of these pretty fellows, I'll be bound. You can be sure they already have their escape route planned. What about you? You, Jacob Pawsey, you Ann Buxton, how difficult will it be for the authorities to find you when they need to? While my fine friend here is off and away to some other poor parish to provoke some other gullible souls into further injudicious activity, you will be the ones called upon to answer for your actions - but not just your actions - but his words and actions too!"

The crowd has become quite quiet now. People are listening to him. Thomas Warren knows he will never be a true resident: there are far too many others with greater claim to that. But he is respected. Already he has taught the sons of a number there present. The stick he holds may not be much use as a weapon; probably less as a symbol of his temporary position. Really, what was he expected to do? He might have read the riot act if anyone had thought to furnish him with a copy. Fortunately, he has divided the opposition and feels the sympathy of the majority is now with him. Fortunately there are people there who realise this is getting out of hand but didn't like to say as much. A few minutes earlier, anything might have happened. Now unbelievably, Thomas Warren's eloquence appears to have brought a halt to proceedings.

Henry Robinson knows that the Militia have recently been embodied near Stowmarket and at present are encamped on the Green at Stowupland in anticipation of an exercise planned for the weekend. They are not the most terrifying group of misfits - but alongside the threat of a hangman's noose, the Mid-Suffolk Militia may be enough to disperse the crowd at Stonham mill, if Thomas Warren can only keep them talking.

Some of the Militia are even equipped with ancient flintlock armoury. There have already been a couple of accidents. In the Militia it is your own side you have to fear most. But they know their duty and they can be rapidly on the march, if only Thomas Warren can successfully halt the crowd's advance and keep them talking.

Henry Robinson finds the commanding officer's tent and implants a sense of urgency in the Colonel's mind. Before some have had time to fasten their boots properly, they are quick-marching along the road to Earl Stonham. Away down the road one man is still appealing to the villagers' better nature. If only Thomas Warren can keep them talking!

When the little troop finally arrives, it is to discover the crowd has dispersed and the mill under threat is still intact. Militia-men are sent to a few nearby houses to question the inhabitants, but any memory they might have had of events that evening has mysteriously evaporated into the mild evening air. So the motley band of pretend-soldiers marches back to camp and, but for one thing, matters return to normal.

A note is pushed under the door at the Guildhall the next day. It is poorly written and inexpertly spelt. Any one of his class could do better. *'you told on uss to the milisha you will gett waht is cuming to you.'* It is not signed. It would have been a surprise if it had been. He may not know the name of the letter's author, but others clearly do. People start to ignore him. People who have always passed the time of day whenever they meet him now cross the road to avoid speaking. So he asks around and finds that Jacob Pawsey has put the word out. Thomas Warren has been a snake in the grass and is to be 'put to it.' Except Thomas Warren knows only too well this is unjustified in the extreme.

So he calls at Pawsey's home. He is shown into the one room other than the kitchen on the ground floor. Jacob Pawsey sits sullen in his chair.

"If you have something to say about me, I would rather you said it to my face, Jacob."

"You grassed us," he replies sulkily.

"I most certainly did not. How was I supposed to do that when I was standing in front of you the whole time?"

"You sent that boy: Robinson's boy."

"I knew nothing about it. He was worried and went looking for help. And don't think you can take this out on him. He showed more sense than the lot of you put together. Claiming the miller had a secret store of corn! I ask you. Look at that crumbling heap of a building. Where is he supposed to keep it? He struggles to accommodate the corn that comes in for milling. You can't keep bags of corn in a place like that. If he did have it the rats would have eaten it by now. Have some sense man. Be honest and admit it, you got it wrong. Now, I want something done about my good name. You have blackened it and nobody will give me the time of day. I wouldn't be surprised if the only boy I have to teach in a fortnight's time is John Coats, seeing as how you have got at all the labourers in the village."

"I s'pose I'm sorry then."

"Well thank you very much, but that unfortunately is not good enough."

"So what am I s'posed to do."

"You and whoever pulled your strings will take out an advertisement in the Journal saying how sorry you are and how wrong you are and how my being 'put to it' was a mighty mistake."

Jacob Pawsey thinks a moment, nods, then sits back in his chair, clearly embarrassed by the whole sorry business. To be honest, Warren doesn't believe for a moment Jacob Pawsey will go as far as he has requested, but so long as he undoes what he has started, that will be enough.

However, two weeks later, a copy of Friday's Journal is pushed under his door. Halfway down the second column of the back page is the promised announcement.

This is to inform the PUBLICK
that I, JACOB PAWSEY of Earl Stonham, Suffolk
having information given me of a false report
regarding THOMAS WARREN being an informer,
do hereby declare the same to be false and without foundation

JACOB PAWSEY

Who paid for its publication and who corrected Jacob Pawsey's wayward English is anybody's guess, but at least he has been as good as his word.

Chapter 11 ~ Towards Winter 1765

Slowly things have returned to normal. Flour prices have adjusted themselves downwards and though they grumble among themselves, the labouring classes take their poverty in their stride as Autumn hastens toward Winter. Slowly, those people reluctant to acknowledge Thomas Warren, once more mumble insincere greetings as they pass him in the churchyard on a Sunday morning. Slowly they begin to accept he was only doing his job - an unpleasant one at the best of times - a job they would not have been prepared to do themselves. The new workhouse at Barham has been completed. It being no longer necessary to deputise for the parish constable, Thomas Warren has been relieved of that duty and can give his new class his undivided attention. If only that were so.

Candler Bird pays him a visit. Such visits have been few and far between in recent months, but today he is back.

"I never did really thank you for what you did this Summer," he begins.

"Things seem to have calmed down, but you have the opening of the Union House to deal with first."

"People will see it is a change for the better. They need to trust us more."

"That as I see it, is the problem," says Warren. "They may have trusted you and your colleagues when it was down to you to do what was best for our people. But now in their eyes you are casting them out: handing the parish's problems over to some unknown and untrusted other entity. Can't you understand. They aren't rioting because they are poor or even because they're hungry. The people of Suffolk are rioting because they are afraid."

"Afraid of what? Death?"

"No, not death so much as what comes before it. Up till now, our parish has looked after its own. Someone gets too old to care for themselves, we house them and make sure someone goes in each day to feed them. If a single girl gets pregnant and can't make the father face up to his responsibilities, then we do something about that. Earl Stonham, not some Union of parishes who don't even know who she is. If parents have a child that will always be less than perfect - lame, feeble-minded or deaf - they worry what will happen to that child when they die or become in need of care themselves. They used to trust us to act on their behalf. And we did! I have looked in your Overseers' accounts and I'll tell you something, I am impressed. Just eighty years ago, a poor blind boy by the name of George Wells was trained at this parish's expense to be instructed in the art of music and singing so he had a chance, in spite of his disability, to earn a living. Would we do that today? Or would we send the poor child off to the workhouse to compete for scraps with the old and the insane."

Thomas Warren looks Candler Bird full in the face and dares him to justify what is being done in the name of mercy.

"I think..." Candler tries to explain, "...that you have an inaccurate understanding of the nature of the Union House. Have you read the brief that has been published in the Journal about the way it must be run? It is to be a refuge for all of the most needy in our parishes, a place of shelter, supplying food, warm clothing and a clean, healthy home: an opportunity for even the most sick to make a small contribution through the medium of work: a Christian place with its own curate and its own chapel. Believe me, I wouldn't put my faith in a system that hadn't been created for the finest of ideals."

"Oh, Can, I honestly believe you mean well, but there are thirty-four parishes in this Union. Surely you can see how there will never be the same consideration given to our people under your new system. Think man! Old Ezekiel Blomfield thought he would finish his days in one of our town houses. I'll wager that as soon as your Union House opens its doors, he, along with anyone else in the parish that is too much trouble, will be whisked away out of our sight. Ann Tooke and her bastard; Robert Bolton whose parents cannot much longer care for a man with a mind like a child; the Hogger children whose mother is dying. You see, they will be the victims of your system built around high ideals. And they will suffer - for as long as they last."

"I'm sorry Thomas, but the decision is made. We have made our first contribution to the furnishing of the place. A Governor has been appointed. We shall use the facility as little as we can, but we *shall* use it."

"Then I think you need to explain it to the people of the parish. Tell them of your high ideals. Convince them it will be a change for the better. Calm their fears. For they are afraid. And I believe, though I'll not say it to them, that their fears are very much justified."

All this has taken place one Sunday morning after church. The schoolboys have attended matins as usual, departing to enable the more fastidious mothers to launder their uniforms ready for school the following day. Candler Bird has one further observation to make.

"I see the Palmer girl is still in attendance," he remarks.

"Indeed and I am glad of her help," says Thomas Warren.

"People are bound to talk."

"Let them."

"You are not worried that gossip might affect her reputation as well as your own?"

"We can't let our lives be dominated by the petty-minded ignorance of others."

"Yet you expect me to bow to other people's fear of the unknown?" Mr. Bird is still concerned by the schoolmaster's lack of support for his social revolution.

"I am just one person, as are you. Perhaps we both need to make the purity of our intentions clear."

There is no immediate answer to that but, mulling over their conversation, Candler Bird will arrange a meeting to present to the parish population a more positive declaration of the way things are going to be from now on. This meeting will not be advertised beyond the parish. It will go unreported and unminuted as, officially, no such meeting has taken place.

Unfortunately, a man such as Mr. Bird does not always possess the common touch. That is to say, what he perceives as positives are not necessarily those advantages most valued by members of the labouring class. Had he focused on three-square-meals-a-day and left it there, he might have swayed opinion a little. However, telling folk they are to be treated regularly for lice and having their rooms regularly fumigated with wormwood offers less by way of appeal. The separation of the sexes, regardless of marital status, is not well received. Even fresh soap and linen once a month comes some way down their mental list of priorities for life. The 'able poor', by which Candler Bird means every person above the age of five years, will not be overjoyed to learn that their labour is to be from six in the morning until seven in the evening. Much mention is made of the orderly and well-behaved. Candler Bird tries to give the impression that soon the Union House at Barham will be housed by grateful and contented people. It is amazing that anyone would still want to live in their own home.

Except, as the schoolmaster could have predicted, nobody believes a word of what he has to say. Too much news has already come from elsewhere. And none of it good.

It will be most of another year before the first influx of 'visitors' to the Barham Union House takes up residence. In the meantime, Thomas Warren has a class to teach. The three new boys seem awfully young and dreadfully slow, but he knows this is mainly down to the fact that two years have been spent with the same group uninterrupted. The class of '65 had little chance of matching up to the class of '63, '64. And there is still the added bonus of Martha who has truly blossomed. No longer a pretty girl; now a delightful young woman with charm in abundance. No wonder people talk!

He has not heard from George Buckle. Now that is a disappointment. He had always felt that he and George had a... a connection. Of all the boys he has taught, there was something special about his relationship with George. More than his relationship with his own two children to be honest. He would have thought that of all of them it would be George who would have maintained contact. But nothing! Not a word. Of course his step-brother William is in the class now and he passes on such news as he has to impart. London is exciting, noisy; the work is hard, both physically and mentally. But he thrives upon such challenges and will do alright for himself. But it would have been nice to have received a letter.

Though there is more to it than that. George is not happy. He is not excited by London. He is not thriving. He does, however, have enough about him to escape a brutal master and find his way all the way home to Stonham. Hungry and footsore, he is gladly received at home. Those responsible for his placement will not be quite so delighted, but it will all pass over. And given time to consider his position, he will be in touch again.

Henry Robinson has written several times and he didn't even need to. He still lives just up the road and the two meet quite regularly, but he seems to take a delight in demonstrating what he has learnt and the letters keep coming. Even Jerry Sharman has quilled a few lines. He, like his father, is a journeyman now, taking work wherever and whenever it is available. Regularly he can be seen accompanying his father to the old Tan Office at Mendlesham Green where the Brotherhood of Friends still meet.

Another year turns around and it brings with it a promise of new life. Beth Warren is pregnant. After over a year of trying, they are successful, it seems. That is to say Beth has what she wants. Thomas Warren is less sure. He finds the two children they already have remote. He is not sure he sees the purpose of adding to them, but if that is what she wants, who is he to think otherwise?

Chapter 12 ~ May 1766

From their home in the Guildhall, the Warrens are perfectly placed to observe the cycle of the seasons. Across the road from their home, cattle and sheep graze the water meadows. Lambs and calves can be heard all the time now. Beyond the Rectory Lane, the field that has lain fallow for the last year has been planted with wheat that is going ahead strongly. There is talk of building in the vicinity, and a sand and gravel pit has been opened beside the road below that selfsame field. Old Southgate is back to shovel what seems like a never-ending supply of gravel onto the church paths. Where does it all go?

The hillside up to Deerbolts remains unploughed and penned pigs are rooting there for such as they can find. Beth and Thomas Warren have quite a flock of chickens and they are back on the lay, though finding the eggs among the mounds in the churchyard is never easy. Somehow the children seem better at it than they are.

It is well into the school year and now they must all face the departure of the rest of what was once the class of '63. Decisions have been made and futures planned. Not every son of a labourer is bound to follow his father back to the land.

James Nunn is to be apprenticed to a blacksmith at Brockford. That is something of a surprise as far as his teacher is concerned. He is certainly not the strongest of boys, nor the most industrious. But he is the most creative and, if he can last the course, it could be the making of him. Smiths do not tend to be the most patient of tradesmen, having a reputation for ill-treating their apprentices. James will have to learn fast to mind his ways and his manners as well as to keep the bellows going.

Isaac Pawsey has an uncle who is a tenant-farmer with no

sons of his own, so he already has a position to take up when school closes for the harvesting. In much the same way, John Coats will join his father on their farm in Stowupland.

Tom Brett has been offered and spurned the opportunity to better himself. Keen to drag at least one of the Brett children out of their endless cycle of poverty, a place had been found in Woodbridge apprenticing him to a tallow-chandler. But oddly, the little lad who has never held tight to an opinion of his own is utterly certain this is not for him. He refuses to go, and nothing anyone says will change his mind. The place goes to another. Thomas will stay in Earl Stonham for the time being, labouring the same fields as his father and his grandparents before him.

It is not good news. Oh, his mother will be pleased enough to keep him there; to send him out into the fields to earn a few pence a week scaring birds off the crops or picking stones out of the way of the ploughshares. But there will be adverse comments. There always are. Thomas Warren has heard them before. There will again be those who will say that's what you get for educating the sons of labourers. Ideas! They get ideas. Above themselves! What is the point?

As for Samuel Tricker, now there's a surprise. Who would have believed he had the confidence to do what he has done? Of all the class he seemed the least likely to make his own decisions and to act on them. More solid Suffolk labouring stock - nothing wrong with that. But imaginative, inventive, with ideas to match? Surely not! But Samuel Tricker, of all the boys of that class will be the one to travel farthest and achieve the most, even if he does end up close to where he started.

Rather than wait for others to determine his future, aged just ten, he has walked to Stowmarket and talked Shadrach Manning, the owner of one of the largest malting companies in the town into employing him in the office. He can cast accounts and write letters and logs as well as most with double the education. What is more, he is determined he will not work the land as have generations before him. He has worn clothes supplied to him by somebody else for the last three years. He will not feel uncomfortable being clothed appropriately by Mr. Manning, who has taken rather a liking to this brash youngster in his charge.

So soon, all of the class of '63 will have gone their separate ways, some leaving families behind, their only reminder of their years in school being a Bible presented on their departure by the Trustees and bearing an inscription in their own hand promising to pay for it should they ever make their fortune.

Beth Warren is again unwell. This has not been an easy confinement. Not like the last two who thrived in the womb and popped out in minutes like corks from bottles of ale. Martha Palmer has been a godsend. She is there most of the time now, and she is needed. Thomas can hardly teach his class and look after his own two. If either of his own children showed any inclination to learn, he could include them in the class, but the boy who bears his own name will have none of it. And the daughter, Elizabeth just cries for her mother - or for Martha. For it is Martha who is as much of a mother to those children as anyone right now.

"Mr. Warren, I think you should come right quick."

That is Martha, one warm day in May when he and his class have been struggling to ignore Beth Warren's groans overhead. Leaving the boys, Thomas Warren follows the girl up the stairs to the small room under the eaves where his wife has taken up residence. Frightened and upset, their two children cling to their mother.

"Take Tom and Liz downstairs. I'll sit with her awhile. Tell the boys to finish their tasks and take themselves away home for today," Thomas Warren says. Martha follows these instructions.

Beth's voice is soft and feeble. "When I die, you'll be able to marry her," she says.

"Don't be a fool, you'll not die. The baby'll come and

you'll be fit and well again."

But she doesn't look as if she will. Something is wrong this time. Something needs doing. For once in his life he feels things are outside his control. All he can do is hope that someone else might have the answer, for he cannot imagine that there is no answer.

"I'll send for Doctor Palgrave."

"No, we cannot afford his fees."

"We cannot afford to leave you and our child at risk," he says, and he means it. He is genuinely worried. For the next ten minutes, little more is said. There is not a lot to say. He has made her as comfortable as he can. But he can't ignore her pain and distress for ever.

"Martha, can you come here, please," he calls. There are footsteps on the stairs.

"The boys have gone, all except for Will Tydeman whose mother will collect him," says Martha.

"Thank you. Now please could you grant us another favour. We need you to fetch Doctor Palgrave. Hire a horse from the Brewery Tap." He finds coins in a purse attached to his belt. "And please hurry." Martha needs no further telling and giving the two Warren children a kiss as she leaves, she runs down the road as fast as her boots and billowing skirts allow.

It seems forever before the surgeon arrives. The last schoolboy has been collected, the Warren children have been fed by their father in an attempt to bring a little cheer to their grim faces. Thomas has tried to blot from his hearing his wife's moans. But when he lifts her covers to make her more comfortable, he is horrified to see just how swollen she is. This is more than a pregnancy. Women grow large with a child at such times, but not like this. Only the severest dropsy could account for her present state. He looks helplessly at the Home Medical book still sitting unopened on a shelf. A lot of use that will be now! No wonder his poor wife has taken to her bed. No wonder her cries drown out all other sounds. No wonder she fears for her life. Now, so does he.

When the surgeon finally arrives in horse-drawn gig, he is a little ahead of Martha who has returned her horse to its owner. "What will he do? The surgeon. Will he make her well? Do we need the midwife?" Martha, usually so composed, is like a lost child.

"I don't know, but I do fear something is unusually awry." He does not tell Martha what he has seen. Soon enough, the surgeon is back downstairs talking to them. He looks grim and the news he has to impart is no more encouraging.

"I shall need a bowl - a large one. I need to release water from her abdomen. I can hear nothing of the child. I think you must prepare yourself for a difficult time. It is your wife I must try to care for now, and even she may be beyond my expertise."

The bowl is found and, together with the tools of his trade, Doctor Palgrave goes to administer whatever he may by way of relief. Something is hopeful. Beyond one small cry of pain, Beth Warren's groans become fewer and quieter; that at least is a relief for all concerned. But when the surgeon reappears, it is not to put their minds at rest.

"She is calmer and more comfortable. You will discover the bowl is full of water mixed with a little blood. There was more than it could contain and I am afraid the bed and floor are somewhat damp. As I feared, the child is dead within her and may have festered there. I can only hope that her body will eject it and begin its recovery. I would have let a little blood, but she is too weak and besides, enough bad-humoured blood passed out with the water."

The surgeon gathers his bags and carries them to his gig. Then he departs with a promise to return the following day. His bill will follow. Martha is persuaded to go home. Thomas would rather she were there, but he knows his wife would not.

On Friday 30th May, Thomas Warren together with his two children will climb the path to St. Mary's Church to attend the funeral of their mother, his wife. All who can attend do. Some to offer condolence, some to cast a glance at Martha Palmer and wonder. The coffin will be placed in an unmarked grave between that of Francis Whistlecroft and later, Joseph Blomfield, two people she never had a lot of time for. But few of us can choose the company we keep in the graveyard.

The school year threads its way through the flourishing, the ripening and on to the gathering in. The last of the class of '63 receive their Bibles and head out to find their fortunes or merely to await whatever comes their way. Although her cousin is no longer a pupil at the school, perhaps the master should not be surprised to find he still has an assistant. Martha Palmer comes on the first morning of school after harvest and returns every day after that. One Friday late in September, she is slow to leave and stays to cook them both a supper. She will not make her way to the school on Monday morning. She will already be there. Now let them talk!

Yet it is not as quick and shameless as it appears. The Warren children need caring for, and their father has been finding it hard. Martha will give of her best: she is closer in age to them than she is to their father and feels a little sorry for them in spite of their sullen ways. Friday night, she cuddles up to them and sleeps a fitful sleep, the children wriggling about on either side of her. That Saturday evening, young Tom and Lizzy are taken by their grandfather to stay the night at Wix Green. Now the two consenting adults are, for the first time, alone and unrestrained. Except they are both extremely inhibited when it comes down to it. For so long, any feelings either might have felt for the other have had to be smothered. Thomas Warren has only ever been close to one woman, so passion is something of which he has remarkably little experience. As for the girl herself, confused by this sudden opportunity, she has no inkling of how things should progress.

So, there is a lot of talking, a smothering of kisses and the first tentative touchings. After that they both know where this is heading, albeit slowly. There will be special times that will hang on the memory... a travelling theatre show, Christmas with the whole Palmer family, and long walks together as a new spring brings with it longer lighter warmer evenings.

One particular day in late April, they walk together up the road where he leads her to a path that follows a bushy field-margin before it dog-legs up the hill across a meadow. At the top, they pause. Looking back, they find the hedgerows are not simply green. There is every colour on show from yellow through oranges to the deepest of forest greens. Cattle are lowing in the water meadows beneath and they are completely surrounded by sheep. St. Mary's Church dominates their view of that little corner of the world, and it is warm and encouraging.

Barely a few dozen further steps are taken before they find themselves in Fen Lane, a dusty meandering road that seems to lead from nowhere to nowhere. There are not a lot of dwellings to be seen in Fen Lane and even fewer people. Farther down, an overgrown footpath takes them beside a muddy ditch and they follow it to the river and the fen where rushes grow and snipe nest. Anyone walking this path may be lucky enough to find a makeshift bridge has been created from a plank or two, but they don't last long and for most passing this way, if they are to progress further, they have to launch themselves across the stream. This how it is for Thomas and Martha: they run-up and jump, and try to remain upright on landing so they don't touch their hands down into the nettles covering the opposite bank.

They cross the field beside Woolney Hall, the most

impressive house on the circuitous walk. It has been there a long time; who knows how long. Not far from here, back in the mists of time, a few French monks once set up camp, calling it a Priory. It probably never amounted to much, and it disappeared far sooner than King Henry's ridding of the monasteries, Thomas tells Martha as they cross the field towards the road grandly named 'The Lord's Highway'. They have to step carefully around cow-pats, left as traps to catch the unwary.

'The Lord's Highway', for all its exalted title, is just a dirt track that follows the river terrace and leads down out of Creeting into Earl Stonham. Which Creeting? Now there's a question! Once there were four, now it seems, only three. There are certainly only three churches left, but old locals will inform you that 'this is the parish of Creeting St. Olaves', remembering a fourth church not far from here that recently went under the plough.

They pass a few rough and unsteady huts - winter shelter for livestock. Up to their right on the hill stands the wood that completely conceals Deerbolts Hall. Then suddenly they spot Earl Stonham church through the trees lining the track, standing proud above the Guildhall and the few gravestones between. There are rabbits everywhere: in the fields, on the bank, even along the track. Thomas makes a dart at one, but it is far too quick for him. He knows it can be done. The gipsy boys seem to catch them with ease, but he is just not quick enough. There will be no cony for dinner tonight.

The road, such as it is, plunges down to the stream (or is it a river?) where there is a ford and the challenge of a teetering bridge for those unwilling to get their feet wet. Thomas strides through oblivious: Martha uses the bridge and he mocks her for it.

In July that year, they will marry. And a fine affair it will be. On occasions like this you hope everything will go smoothly, but of course it never does. This time it is officialdom that is to blame. In a way it is William Scapy's fault, but he is a man of little learning, so you can't really lay the problem entirely at his door. Officialdom - that's what comes of marrying such a young girl. Marriage by licence! Requiring the filling-in of forms, countersigned by witnesses. That was William Scapy's role. Mr. Scapy is a man who would probably describe himself as a yeoman; an old-fashioned word, but a fair description of the position and of the man. A farmer who, through industry and endeavour, has kept his immediate family free from the shackles of poverty. A good man - no doubt about it. But in the signing of forms, how was he supposed to realise he was not meant to sign in the space provided for the signature of the groom.

He did, and now the parson is confused, as are the no-longer-so-happy couple. But at the end of the day, the real intention is clear enough. Thomas Warren will marry Martha Palmer. It won't stop an equally confused scribe entering the wrong name in the big book where such information is entered and stored. So what? Nobody will ever look at it again, will they?

The marriage proceeds without further hitches and afterwards over a glass or two of wine supplied by the bride's father, the new husband tells Candler Bird and any others who care to listen that this is for the sake of his children who desperately need a replacement mother. But...

"You can say that as often as you like," Candler Bird tells him, "...but we only need to cast a look at that young lady to see what replacement service she is providing." This is forthright even by Candler's standards. A blunt instrument if ever there was one. But they can speak to one another like that now. And Thomas has his answer.

"And the age difference between you and your wife is...? Oh yes, five years greater than my new wife and myself. Or has my grasp of mathematics deserted me?"

"I think not, neither has your grasp of a pretty young woman. How, I ask myself, did an old goat like you inveigle such a little beauty into marriage?"

"Charm, Mr. Bird, charm," chuckles Thomas. "Some have it, some have not."

"My guess is she thinks there's a pot of gold under your bed. You know the old rhyme?"

"No; which one might that be?" asks Thomas, knowing full well the verse he is about to repeat.

"The girls of this age are so dazzled with show,
When they're scheming to settle in marriage,
That to the church with the Devil they gladly would go
If the Devil would give them a carriage."

Candler Bird smirks as if this were the most original piece of poetry ever produced at such an event. It is far from that but Thomas gives him his moment of delight. Just long enough for him to slip in the next predictable remark.

"So when can we expect a christening?" he asks.

"In all likelihood it'll be slightly longer delayed than the christening of your first child was, I suspect."

Yes, Thomas Warren can even get away with a comment like that now. Just as long as they keep the banter between themselves. That's how it is between the best of friends. That is how it is meant to stay, until...

Chapter 13 ~ October 1767

Promises are hard to keep when, in spite of their being made with the best of intentions, you are reliant on other people to see them through. So it is that the schoolmaster, acting on advice from Billy Last, the father of one of his class, is to pay a visit to the Union house at Barham. The Workhouse, as it is known to most, has been open to the poor of the Bosmere and Claydon Hundred for about a year, and trust of the place locally has not improved. All the Overseers' comforting assertions are said, by those who claim to know, to be a sham. Now Thomas Warren wants to know the truth and he is aware that this may involve a few unfortunate, but wholly necessary untruths and deceptions.

'Catch them early,' he has been advised, 'and they'll think it is official.' Early in the morning is when Parish Overseers and Government Inspectors pay their infrequent calls.

Up well before the crack of dawn, he forces himself awake and harnesses Martha's pony. A journey of about eight miles will take him along the turnpike towards Needham Market, then through the woodland of Shrubland Park towards Barham. The first frosts of autumn are now appearing. If he felt sleepy when he started out, by the time he is skirting Coddenham, he is wide awake and pulling his coat tight around him.

The Union House stands close to the Sorrell Horse, just five miles short of Ipswich. It is an ugly building with high walls and an impressive gateway at the front. It might equally well be a prison. Thomas makes his presence known and is taken directly to the Master of the house. Now the first lie.

"I have been sent by the Stonham Overseers to review our use of this facility." He doesn't say which of the three Stonhams he represents and he isn't asked. The Governor is not a local man and still hasn't come to terms with the geography of the area. Instead, keen to please, the man leads him down dreary stinking corridors into rooms that are so thinly furnished it is hard to determine their purpose, and ever on to places where something akin to food is being slopped into bowls. There are rooms where all are supposed to be put to work of some sort - spinning, grinding of cattle bones for manure, the mixing of lime-wash to paint the so-far unfinished interiors. It is not just depressing, it is horrific. And it makes him angry, but not half as angry as he will be when he is given access to the book of admissions.

The Governor of the Bosmere and Claydon Union House takes a pride in his paperwork. Meticulously, records are kept. Each name is painstakingly entered. Every date of an arrival, and of a departure, for whatever reason. What this man fails to grasp is just how revealing those records he has so lovingly maintained might be to one such as Thomas Warren.

The schoolmaster from Earl Stonham is a mild-mannered man. He does not often lose his temper. But when he does, folks had better beware! With people like that, it is as if they are saving it all up for the one big moment. One big moment! This is it!

At Deerbolts, a powerful low sun streams through easterly-facing windows. Candler Bird is not an early riser any more. Not since he celebrated his sixtieth year on this earth. So he is still enjoying a leisurely breakfast when he is disturbed by a visitor he wasn't expecting.

"Have you any idea? Did you know it was going to be like this? Do you care? Were you just blind to what was bound to happen, or were you lying through your teeth to our people from the start?"

"Thomas, what a nice surprise. Have you eaten yet?"

"Yes," he shouts aloud. "I have eaten: simply, but undoubtedly better than those poor souls in that... place!" Now Candler is beginning to detect a hint of what he is railing about.

"Have you by any chance been to our new Union House at Barham?" Candler asks. "I know it is not exactly what you or I would describe as comfortable. But you make it too luxurious and the undeserving and the feckless will be queuing up for hand-outs."

"But have you seen the registers?" the schoolmaster asks. "Have you really looked at the story that is building up around that vile creation of yours?"

"To be honest, not exactly my doing. I know it has its failings - a few teething problems, doubtless. But the men and women there are fed and clothed. They are clean and safe and, what is more, they have the opportunity to give something back in the way of honest Christian work."

"Mark my words, there is nothing Christian about that place," Warren continues. "I have seen for myself. I kept my peace whilst you spun your comforting words before the people of this parish. But I can keep my peace no longer."

"I would be interested to know by which device or means you have been able to examine the books at the Union House."

Ah, now that might be a bit more tricky to explain. But by now Thomas Warren is in full flow and in full command of the figures. Those most damning of statistics!

"Do you know how many poor souls were admitted to the workhouse at the time it was opened?"

"Oh, a hundred or so. The building was designed to hold at least double that." To be honest Candler Bird has not a clue. He only knows that their parish, to justify the expense to which they had been put, sent six of their most desperate and destitute.

"Two hundred and sixty-six were admitted last year, and they didn't open their doors until October."

"Well, there was bound to be a flurry of activity with it being new and all."

"Do you know how many of those poor wretches are no longer alive?"

Of course he doesn't. He doesn't even know that four of the Earl Stonham six are now dead, the other two remaining alive only because they ran away.

"Eighty-seven. Eighty-seven of the first overcrowded intake didn't even make it through the first winter. Now don't try to tell me they were all sick. If so, they were in no fit state to be moved there in the first place. Just you think on it. Eighty-seven; four of them our own. And that is just the ones who entered those gates last year. Please don't try to tell me it is getting better. Safe, you said. They would be safe and cared for. They would have had a better chance of survival in my garden shed! When people hear the truth about that place, they will again rise up and tear it down. And so they should!"

"Thomas, you can't make this public. All confidence in the system would evaporate. We need this. Yes, it needs to be managed better, but the parishes simply cannot afford to run things the way they used to. It is the future. Before long, every Hundred in Suffolk will have a Union House. We may have to learn a few lessons about how the sick and the elderly should be cared for, but it has to be like this; only with better results."

What Thomas expected from this revelation he is not sure. Perhaps he thought Candler Bird would be as horrified as he still is. Maybe he envisaged the pair of them going back to Barham on a mission of mercy to free the unfortunates incarcerated there. Had he thought that, he is to be bitterly disappointed. If this shocking news is indeed news to Mr. Bird, it does not appear to have provoked much by way of a response.

Candler's cool calmness is having an effect. Thomas Warren's anger is running out of impetus, and that is precisely what Candler Bird is relying on.

"You are such a radical, Thomas. We clearly need you to be

our conscience. Or to jog ours into activity. Trust me and the other Overseers. We shall investigate your claims and, be assured, something will be done, if not immediately, then as fast as possible."

Comforting words. But there have been so many comforting words. If the truth be known, Earl Stonham cannot afford to pay thirty pounds a quarter towards the upkeep of the workhouse and not use it. So other poor souls will be placed there, however much the vociferous few protest. But quietly. It is better to hide such matters from those who might object. Thomas Warren has been allowed a glimpse of their 'future' and now look at the state of things! Fortunately he has had his moment. For the time being.

As for change, the Governor will be reprimanded for permitting 'all and sundry' to see the books without written authority. Doctors will be called a little more often to the dying. But the graveyard at Barham will continue to fill with unmarked and unremembered corpses. And, bringing it all a bit closer to home, the workhouse at Barham will be 'home' at one time or another to Thomas Brett's sister Sarah, as well as cousins of Henry Robinson, Jerry Sharman, George Buckle and James Nunn. Not necessarily the most wretched in the parish: possibly the most expendable.

Number	Persons entered into the House: Persons Names	Aged Yrs	What Parish	When admitted	Persons Dead or Discharged: Persons Names	When Dead or Discharged	How Disposed of
				1766			
1	Mary Level	20	Coddenham	Revd Mr Jn Bacon	Mary Level	May 30: 1769	Run away
2	Ann Level	19	Do		Ann Level	Oct 12. 1767	Run away
3	Sarah Lord senr	25	Henley	Revd Mr Lawrence	Sarah Lord Senr	Mar 9. 1767	Discharged
4	Sarah Lord junr	10	Do		Sarah Lord junr	Do Do	Do
5	Mary Wilson	55	Ashbocking	Rev Mr Rich Brown	Mary Wilson	Novr 27th 1775	Dead

Entered into the House in a regular Form according to the proposed manner of receiving them October 3d

Number	Persons Names	Aged Yrs	What Parish	When admitted	Persons Names	When Dead or Discharged	How Disposed of
6	James Cooke	77	Little	Do	James Cooke	Apl 23. 1767	Dead
7	Francis Ford	50	Stonham	Do	Francis Ford	Apl 30. 1767	Do
8	Mary Balls	35	Barking		Mary Balls	Decr 28. 1766	Dead
9	Philip Balls	5	Do	Do	Philip Balls	Octr 12th 1775	Discharged
10	Dennis Balls	9 mos	Do	Do	Dennis Balls	Jan 13. 1767	Dyed
11	Martha Hill	61	Do	Do	Martha Hill	Sept 6	Dead
12	Mary Bagley	80	Do	Do	Mary Bagley	March 28. 1767	Dead
13	Bridget Webb	84	Do	Do	Bridget Webb	Dec 11 68	Do
14	Rachel Fosdick	33	Do	Do	Rachel Fosdick	Oct 14 1766	Discharged
15	Rach Fosdick Jun	9	Do	Do	Rach Fosdick Jun	Do	Do
16	Mary Fosdick	5	Do	Do	Mary Fosdick	Do	Do
17	Ann Fosdick	1	Do	Do	Ann Fosdick	Do	Do
18	Ann Ward	13	Do	Do	Ann Ward	June 20th 1769	Do
19	Susan Ramsey	11	Do	Do	Susan Ramsey	July 5th 1769	Do
20	Ann Vincent	13	Do	Do	Ann Vincent	Augt 9. 1768	Discharged
21	Ann Eastwick	10	Do	Do	Ann Eastwick	Augt 17. 1770	Do
22	Susan Boore	60	Do	Do	Susan Boore	July 28. 1768	Dead
23	Mary Ward	8	Do	Do	Mary Ward	May 9th 1772	Discharged
24	Willm Goldsbury	85	Do	Do	Willm Goldsbury	Sept 13. 1768	Dead
25	Saml Ward	83	Do	Do	Saml Ward	Decr 21. 1766	[illegible]
26	Danl Eastwick	11	Do	Do	Daniel Eastwick	Augt 17. 1770	Discharged
27	Peter Wright	10	Do	Do	Peter Wright	Sep 20. 1769	Discharged
28	Wm Farthing	68	Do	Do	Wm Farthing	May 24: 1767	Dead
29	Thom Neve	74	Do	Do	Thomas Neve	Jan 17. 1767	Discharged
30	George Baker	13	Do	Do	Geo: Baker	March 18th 1768	Run away
31	Saml Ward	12	Do	Do	Sam. Ward	Oct 13. 1767	Discharged
32	Mary Vince	60	Earl Stonham	October ye 4th	Mary Vince	Feb 14th 1777	Dead
33	William Fisher	73	Do	Do	Wm Fisher	June 8 1767	Do
34	Ezekiel Blomfield	88	Do	Do	Ezekl Blomfield	July 1st 67	Do
35	Robt Boston	24	Do	Do	Robt Boston	Sep 4. 1770	Do
36	Massey Hogger	11	Do	Do	Massey Hogger	Oct 29. 1770	Discharged
	[illegible] Hogger			Do	Ann Hogger	Dec 30. 1770	Run away

Chapter 14 ~ 1768

"Legal! Legitimate! Well, there's two words I never expected to hear spoke in this house."

Fair comment. Which all goes to show how surprised Mary Pawsey is to hear her husband's latest suggestion.

"You hen't let me explain."

"No need; it's all a loada squit. Jus' wishful thinkin'."

"Thirty acres. We can make a livin' by farming, like others do. But it comes at a price, an' I don't jus' mean the rent."

After years of supplementing a precarious living working on the land with a little bit of poaching, Jacob Pawsey is now contemplating something of a career-change. Thirty acres of prime Earl Stonham land has become available for rent. It is not the ideal time as far as this family is concerned. John at fourteen has the mind of a five year-old. The other two boys are still too young to be much help to their father, but if they can weather the first three or four years, things might get easier. History warns them otherwise. His own grandfather was a tenant-farmer in the parish until a succession of bad years put paid to his ambition.

There are further difficulties to consider. In addition to the fifteen pounds a year for the rent, there will be a fine payable on the drawing-up of the indenture. But more to the point, Jacob will be known no more as a mere labourer: they will become farmers. Farmers don't go night-adventuring. No more poaching!

"But, folks come to us to get stuff they can't get otherwise; even legal, legitimate folks like Mr. Bird." That is true. At least it has been: no questions asked, supply and demand.

Mary Pawsey knows what he's like when he gets hold of an idea, but she's not finished yet.

"Alright, you're suggestin' we jus' work for a livin', I

s'pose. When have you ever been able to feed this family by the sweat of your brow. Look around you. There's plenty have tried that, only to end up in the workhouse. An' how you gonna arrange it all? You gotta find money as down-payment, pay workers and buy stock, on top of which you say poachin's gotta stop. Don't make sense!"

It won't be easy, he knows that. He is no longer as young as he used to be and he'll demand far more dedication from himself than any employer ever had from him. But it is an opportunity for the boys' sake as much as any other. This will be about the whole family working together. There are limits to what John will ever achieve. Isaac is only twelve, but he is growing. Abraham is ten, but if he stops attending school, he too can play his part. Even Susan can milk cows, feed hens; put up fences if necessary. They can learn to shear sheep and spin wool and all manner of tasks. Jacob remembers a discussion he had ten years earlier with Thomas Brett. He had a chance like this and had to decline. Fifty acres, that was. Old man Garnham, his father-in-law could no longer work it and he was given first refusal. But a refusal it had to be. And he has regretted it ever since.

So patiently, he explains to the whole family why he intends to go ahead with this. Isaac, listening quietly, is secretly excited by the prospect. Jacob tells his wife and children just what will be expected from them. The unspoken corollary to all this being... if only our boy, Jacob had lived. He would now be twenty. But, by the grace of God, five years ago he had changed over a few weeks from a strong healthy lad to a corpse. If only...

Having explained *why*, he now moves on to the *how*.

"I can delay the payment of the fine and the first rental. Mr. Hicks say it can wait to enable us to get started, but there will be expenses, before we see a lot of return. We take occupation of the land after Michaelmas, so we get to put by as much as we can from this harvest."

They all know what that means. Work whatever hours they can and squirrel away every penny.

"In the meantime, there will be one last night out, if you see what I mean. We in't gonna poach no more after this, so we owe them rich buggers something to remember us by, me an' you two boys."

And as usual, he has it all planned. Each year at the beginning of November, the Great and the Good of Earl Stonham and Creeting All Saints will meet to celebrate Guy Fawkes night with a feast. This year, it is their parish's turn to act as hosts. A large quantity of birds will be required. Local farmer John Hicks knows who to ask. Capons is what he says he wants but, plucked and drawn, he won't know the difference, will he? The two men have already agreed this should be the last time they do this kind of business together.

It is that time of night when, if a curfew actually tolled the knell of parting day in Earl Stonham, it would be long past. In the Pawsey house, this is all they have spoken about for weeks. Outside the house, not a word! They need more money than they have ever had before, so to supplement their expected return from working the long hours of harvest-season, this will be one last big night out, Jacob and his two younger sons, Isaac and Abe.

Then... legal and legitimate: there's something rather fresh and enticing about that. Even their mother is coming round to the idea. No more worries about being hired, because they will be the ones doing the hiring. Eventually. But all that is in the future. Right now it is all about feeding a family of six from what can be produced in just thirty acres. So whenever Isaac's imagination starts to get the better of him, his father brings him back down to earth with, "Huh, ideas above yourself, young Isaac. Must be that school you went to."

"You went there too."

"Only for a year - t'was all we could afford then."

"But old Ling taught you to read."

"An' a fat lotta good it's done me."

"...So far, but you must've been glad to read them leases and indentures - see that bit of schoolin' did you some good."

"Oh, I'll admit I mighta done better - I weren't the most attentive, but what I come away with was worth the effort."

Working together for themselves has brought father and son closer than they have ever been. The task they have set themselves is not an impossible one. Within a mile or two of them are at least four men successfully tilling land for themselves who began their working lives as labourers.

They know they are unlikely ever to get rich from the labour of others, and they know they are working harder than they ever have in their lives. Which is why the little sidelines have to go. This family cannot afford to have one or more of them in gaol, or worse. So this will most definitely be the last time.

It is over a week before the November 5th feast. The birds will be all the better for hanging that long. Added to which, it is all part of the plan. Gipping Great Wood lies about three miles north-west from where they live. It is Tyrell land, and poaching there is not for the faint-hearted. Keepers with guns and hounds patrol the rides at night. But it is a place where an intrepid poacher can guarantee to come away with a substantial haul.

There has been a wedding at the big house and celebrations will continue well into the night. It would not be surprising had his Lordship thought to leave a bottle or two for his hard-working gamekeepers. Except he hasn't. He wants them to stay alert. However, by arrangement with a friend of the Pawseys, bottles have been left and assumed by the keepers to be a present from a grateful employer. A kind thought, they think.

Meanwhile, under cover of darkness, a small hand-cart has found its way onto the top road above the wood to the East.

Meanwhile, a father and two sons are carefully following a shady hedgerow to bring them within a whisker of the narrow field at the edge of the wood.

They are greeted by a recently-erected notice-board, but it is as dark as an October night can be and they fail to see it warns of man-traps and spring-guns. These are newly-added dangers in addition to those traditionally experienced by night-adventurers such as themselves. It is hard to say whether reading it would have altered their purpose in any way. They plough on. Soon, they know fireworks will be set off at the big house and a few lights and bangs will not come as any great surprise to the slightly inebriated keepers.

Were it not the last big night out of its kind, Jacob Pawsey would normally have left Gipping Wood well alone. But, safely penned away from foxes, the quantity of birds he requires sit plump and ripe for the taking. It is, he would say, too good an opportunity to pass up.

So, whilst others are sleeping off that evening's indulgence, father and sons pick their way through the misty-damp darkness of an Autumn night, clutching a simple hempen net of their own design. The possession of this alone is enough to place all three of them in gaol, should they be spotted, but few are around to see them.

Sacks in hands, the three enter the wood by way of a dry ditch. Dry in summer, that is; but it has rained incessantly for the last week and individually each curses having to start his quest with wet feet.

"Was that barkin'?" Isaac whispers.

"Thass alright; I got meat," his father answers.

What he means is that whilst a bottle or two might pacify the keepers, their dogs might be a different matter. Fortunately, a few bangs carried on the air from the west indicate the party at the big house is in full swing.

"They'll not loose the dogs unless they have to tonight. Take 'em half the night to round'em up again," says Jacob.

In virtually pitch darkness, finding where the birds are penned is no easy feat. The keepers move them around for this very purpose, but a poacher has a nose for such things and guides the boys toward the pen. Isaac is aware this is a real skill that will be abandoned and lost after this night.

Now it is a time for silent stifling - not pretty, just quick and effective. The drawing in of nets of birds and consigning their warm corpses to the sacks, as many as they can comfortably carry.

This is the moment for fear. Sacks filled with their quarry and the dark dread that their every move might be observed. There is the desire to run, to blunder back through the undergrowth as fast as pulling the sacks might permit. Jacob knows how easily it might all go terrifyingly wrong, so whispers calm words encouraging the boys to follow him. To begin with, they stick to the rides, heading for a means of exit. Then as the sounds of barking seem closer, they plunge into the denser darker regions. Autumn has not yet stripped the trees and only vaguely is Jacob aware of a murky-grey lightness that indicates the edge of the wood.

Then, a clang, a shriek, a gasp, a whimper. A father's irritated reminder to keep quiet comes automatically. Realising something untoward and unexpected has happened, he moves to to the source of the sounds. Abe has stopped moving and is caught somehow. He is trying not to cry or call out.

Jacob whispers to Isaac, "Take your sacks to the field and come back for mine. I'll deal with this."

A task trumps fear and paralysis. Isaac is too busy to even wonder what has happened. He returns to take his father's sacks, and then again his brother's. It is beginning to drizzle and, job done, he waits shivering, aware, should a moon appear, he is very much exposed and in the open. But there will not be a moon that night. Not to expose him, nor to give him any indication of what is happening the other side of a charcoal haze.

After what seems forever, his father appears, carrying Abraham, who is softly crying. He has trodden on a man-trap, but he's been lucky. They had laughed at him when he chose to wear his new leather buskins. But they have kept his legs dry and now they have protected his foot. The teeth of the trap have missed his small ankle and scraped the sides of the stiff new leather. It is hard to say whether his leg is broken, but the deadly teeth of the trap have not so much as pierced his skin. Right now they all need to get back to the cart, hopefully with the sacks of birds. Uphill in the wet, this will require two journeys. Then the two fit ones haul the hand-cart along the top lane towards Stowupland.

Jacob has an arrangement with Mr. Coats, his former employer to have the continued use of an old shed to keep his tools until he has time to remove them. This is where the pheasants will be hung and the cart left so, should constables come searching, his own property will be free from the evidence.

Two hours later they stagger in exhausted. Abe is crying louder now there is less danger of being heard, and the leg is certainly a cause for concern. But as suggested, he has been lucky. A chipped bone, no worse, bruises all colours of the rainbow and a limp that will never quite go away. A new nickname - Hoppy. And a battle-scar for which he feels justly proud.

Word comes to Earl Stonham that a raid has been carried out on Mr. Tyrrell's game. The story tells of at least six heavily-armed poachers carrying off over a hundred birds. A gang from Norwich seems most likely.

"Don't look much like capons to me," says John Hicks.

"What do they look like?

"Could be pigeons for all I know."

"B'luddy big pigeons - I tell you, these are the tastiest birds you ever will find.

"Whose are they?"

"Yours, if you pay for'em."

"An' if I don't?" says Hicks.

"Someone else's - plenty would be grateful. And what's more, you wun't have much of a feast next week."

"Fifty birds, you say?"

"Thass right."

"Capons?"

Shrug. "Summat like that."

Such is the way deals are done.

John Coats senior pays Jacob a visit a few days later. He is shown around their small farm, already coming alive with pigs, hens and one solitary cow.

"It's a brave venture you are about to undertake, and I wish you every success. And I take it you will no longer need my old shed... for hanging things in."

Chapter 15 ~ 1773-1777

After some years of requests and complaints, there is good news. The Churchwardens and Overseers have decided to spend money they haven't got. This is all very prodigal of them, but for once they have seen their way clear to investing in the village's future.

The announcement comes in early February as the icicles on the outside of the Guildhall once again reach from eaves to the floor. Bowls are spread around the schoolroom in anticipation of leaks appearing whenever the thaw begins. The building has never been ideal for the purpose to which it has been put for a hundred and fifty years. Now something is to be done about it.

The plan is to build a house at the parish's expense close to the road on Halefield. The better timbers from one end of the Guildhall will be re-used in building it. Once this is built, complete demolition of the Guildhall will begin and then the construction of a new school and workshop.

"So, you see," says John Martin, "We haven't forgotten you down here. Even if it costs a hundred pounds, we intend to see this school continues to thrive."

Fine words, but there is bound to be a catch. There always has been.

"Of course," the churchwarden continues, "...your new accommodation, being a continuing expense to the parish will command a certain... rent."

"Am I to understand you will charge us rent when we have always lived here rent-free. In fact the miserliness of my remuneration is compensated to a certain extent by our having a rent-free home."

"Yes, but I am sure you will understand just how well you

will come out of this. Your new home will give you a level of comfort you have not previously enjoyed. Earl Stonham is having to borrow the money for the work. That may take ten years to pay back, with interest. As your new home will have to serve as a temporary schoolroom whilst the building is completed, we propose to reduce the first year's rent. But after that, a small charge will need to be made."

Mr. Martin is disturbingly imprecise. Who knows what this rent may turn out to be. But it is a relief to have the prospect of a decent home, before the present one falls in. At the moment, that is all the man is prepared to say. 'Well,' thinks Thomas Warren, 'battles over rent can be left until another day.'

Building begins at the edge of Halefield as soon as frosts subside and Thomas and Martha take regular evening strolls a furlong or so up the road to see how work is progressing. Thomas cannot believe his good fortune. His first marriage may not have been as perfect as he had liked. This time, he feels he has a true love-match. Children of their own have still not come their way. Not for lack of trying. In fact, they often laugh to one another how unnecessarily careful they were whilst still unmarried.

The only sadness concerns the children from his first marriage. Never prepared to accept Martha as a replacement mother, they were difficult to say the least. Quite early in the marriage, they moved in with their grandfather, Jeremiah Marsh, and there is little contact between them any more. Young Tom is learning with his grandfather to be a wheelwright. He is starting to develop the physique of a man who works with heavy tools and objects. He never did learn to read, in spite of all his father's encouragement. Grandfather Marsh doesn't mind. Never one for literacy himself, he thinks boys are better off making things with their hands; and he may be right.

Little Lizzy is growing up, and looks every bit of her mother's daughter. She too is probably better off with old man

Marsh, Thomas tells himself. But there remains a certain regret, nevertheless.

Now Thomas has more help with his teaching than ever before. Not only does Martha lend a hand in the schoolroom, but her young nephew John is a regular visitor to the school. He has an assistant teacher's place promised at Framlingham and is seeking to learn more about teaching. He is a keen lad, and the three work well together.

In early summer, Halefield House is complete and the master and his wife have the help of eight boys to carry their possessions and the properties of the schoolroom to their new home. A basket of vegetables sits by the door: a gift from Will Chapman who works the land behind the house. His rent goes some way to paying to keep the school.

Thrilled beyond measure, Thomas and Martha still have room for a tinge of sadness, knowing that their home of the last five years will soon be reduced to a pile of rubble. A few old timbers will be re-used, but most is beyond recovery, and soon all trace of the old Guildhall will be gone.

In its place rises a less impressive but more functional building. Schoolroom at the church-gate end; workshop at the other. Additional accommodation above. Plastered, tiled, water-tight. Everything they ever craved.

However, the rent demanded on Halefield is far more than Thomas and Martha had expected. The parish want in excess of three pounds a year. Out of a salary of just eight pounds. In the end, the first year's rent is eased to a figure of two pounds, sixteen shillings and three pence. How they arrived at that is unclear. But to make up his earnings, Thomas Warren puts the new workshop to use, making all manner of wooden goods that he can sell locally. Guessing that soon enough, he will be charged rent on that too, for the first time in years Warren actively looks about for another teaching position. He has no desire to move from Earl

Stonham. It has many happy associations for him, but his time there is drawing to a close and both he and the Feoffees know it.

John Palmer, Martha's cousin, is now a teacher a dozen miles away in Framlingham. They don't see one another for a while but letters pass between them and news is exchanged. It is in this way that he hears of a position becoming vacant in nearby Debenham. The present master has given notice of his retirement, though the actual date is somewhat vague. This time he receives the support of Candler Bird in his application and he is guaranteed the position at some future, but as yet undefined, date.

Candler Bird's change of attitude shows how the two have warmed to one another as the years have passed. The old man is beginning to show signs of his age. He has slowed down a lot and handed over most of the running of the estate to his elder sons. He is more vague and plays a lesser role in parish affairs than he ever did. In truth, each will miss the other a great deal.

Hearing that Mr. Warren is to move on, one by one and two by three, the boys of '63 pay him visits. Most live close at hand and want to keep in touch. George Buckle brings his young lady to meet the master. George is horseman on a nearby farm and seems to have abandoned all idea of travelling the world. Next to visit are Isaac Pawsey and Tom Brett. Quite the village gents! They both look fashionably attired and are also courting. Then it is John Coats. He still looks fragile for a farmer. Not the build for a man out in all weathers; not made for hard physical labour. But he seems happy enough. Jerry Sharman comes calling. He is still full of ideas, but it is hard to imagine how he might achieve a hint of his potential. He comes looking like a tramp and leaves with some of Thomas Warren's unwanted clothing.

"Well," Martha, says, "You don't want it and it looks like he needs it." There is no doubting that.

Sam Tricker is the complete opposite - smart, almost elegant, you might say, and full of ideas for his future. He comes with James Nunn and Henry Robinson. They have spent the day together and ride to Halefield house in the late afternoon. James, as usual, is quiet, but his eyes sparkle as if he never stops thinking and observing. It is Henry that gives the schoolmaster most cause for concern. There is an air of sadness about him that is hard to understand. Of all the boys, his future seems bright. He taking a leading role in working his grandfather's farm in Combs. Yet, it gives him no delight, that is clear. He too is quiet, but Sam Tricker can talk for the three of them, so there are few pauses in the conversation.

"So when do you expect to be moving on,?" The master is asked for the umpteenth time. It is the one thing each visitor has wanted to know. If only he knew.

It all drags on for over two years, far longer than expected. Finally unable to avoid handing over a class mid-year, Thomas resigns and takes a temporary position teaching with John Palmer in Framlingham until he is advised the time is right for he and his wife to go through the process of applying for an official change of settlement. After all the waiting, they at last make their home in Debenham, where a more acceptable salary, along with a rather grander master's house, free of all rent, have been waiting for them. Briefly, his children join them to assure their new place of settlement. But their time with their father and stepmother is brief. Before long, they have returned to the wheelwright's cottage at Earl Stonham.

The new master at Stonham School is to be Thomas Pizzey, a man more easily moulded in the ways of the village. Certainly not a radical!

Not that his predecessor ever was. Not really. Any suggestion of that, and Debenham would not have entertained the prospect of welcoming him into their midst to be responsible for their children's education. As with Earl Stonham, the Debenham charity school is also supported by a sixteenth-century endowment, but an altogether more generous one than any school-master ever enjoyed in Stonham.

The school is also larger, as twenty poor boys are educated alongside those paying fees to be there. There is the potential for up to three classes. Thomas Warren's first act on his arrival is to appoint his young protégé John Palmer as his deputy.

Chapter 16 ~ late 1777 and after

In 1777, nine burials take place at Earl Stonham. Candler Bird, at the age of 64 is one of them. Another, far younger is John Coats, the first of the class of '63 to succumb to the inevitable. He does not leave a will, but he does voice one last request...

"I don't owe nothin' to nobody and there 'in't many can say that. That is exceptin' I got given a book once, and I meant to do something about it. I writ a promise in the front of that book and I'd like to see it honoured. I don't know what I'm worth, but I reckon that ten pounds they asked for ought to be theirs by right. It's been worth it. That book and the reading of it have been whully useful, I can tell you. So when I'm gone please can you see that it's done."

These words are spoken haltingly, after the service, by John Coats senior, a man broken by the early death of another of his children, but determined to see his son's last wish adhered to. Ten pounds will be duly paid to the school trustees in memory of his son.

After supping tea and ale and rusks and cakes, the remainder of the class of '63 find themselves together in the corner of the room. Some are almost strangers now; others see one another regularly. There is quite a bit of catching up to do. George Buckle has drifted away from his wife who cuddles their new baby protectively. Isaac Pawsey looks surprisingly affluent in his new attire. On the death of his father, he has been able to take over the reins of their small farm, a heavy responsibility for one so young. Nevertheless, he has embraced the challenge with remarkable confidence and says he intends to take on more land soon. It is clear that they have all prospered in their own way.

They'll never be truly wealthy, none of them, but the few years since school have been kind to them and they know what they need to do now. Each and every one of them. For John Coats and for the class to which they all once belonged.

"If John can do that much before he dies at twenty-one, it shouldn't be too much for the rest-on-us to do likewise." That is what George has to say on the matter and, as was always the case, the rest will agree to follow his lead.

Thomas Warren is not able to be there. It is a Friday and too early in his new appointment to be asking for time off. But he has sent his heartfelt commiserations. For the master in his classroom in Debenham, it will be a sombre day. An end to something. A shadow and a loss.

* * * * * * *

Tom Brett is in love. Again. It is not exactly a surprise. Since the age of fourteen he has been declaring his love for young (though not always young) ladies at the rate of about a dozen a year. Some of them even believe him. This time it is different. At least, Eleanor Taylor is different. He tells her he loves her and all she says is, "Yeah, yeah!" As if to say, 'Tell it to the fairies: I've heard it all before!' The trouble is, this time he thinks he means it. She is not the prettiest girl he has ever known, but she has this way about her. She wears her hair short while other girls have it long. She ties her apron in intricate knots as if she means it to stay that way. And she is clever. Tom Brett can still read tolerably and write his name, albeit slowly. But Eleanor is smart in other ways. She has certainly got the measure of him.

Tom's friends have never quite understood his success with the ladies. "After all," says George, "He's not the height of a pocketful of coppers. He looks like a tramp half the time and he'll never amount to much. What do they see in him?"

"They like to mother him," suggests his wife Mary. "Some

women find that helpless look attractive." Then, catching the concerned look on her husband's face, she adds, "Not me of course; I like a man that looks like a man, but I know of plenty that would go for the likes of young Thomas."

There must be something special about Eleanor. He's not so much as looked at another girl for at least... a month? Which is why he is considering asking her to marry him. That and the fact that he knows he'll not get to untie her apron till he does: all of which makes this a prolonged and somewhat uncomfortable courtship, during which time she turns him down repeatedly until... ...until tired of saying no, she relents and agrees to wed him, simple as that.

Just two years after John Coats' death, out at Barking the two make their vows. It is a simple wedding. Tom is one of the few on the farm where he works to be allowed time off for the ceremony, so they choose a day in early March when most workers are preparing and sowing fields near the church, and there is a brief halt in proceedings while colleagues cheer the happy couple, before returning to matters in hand.

Tom Brett seems like a changed man. He feels like a changed man. Being married to Eleanor has worked its magic on him. Before they know it, there is a child on the way and already there are concerns about providing for a family that may grow larger. It is hard decision to leave the only work you know; work that your family has known for generations.

But labouring gets no easier; no more reliable. A bad harvest and you can find you lose your position, your home, your security. Except there is no security. Jerry Sharman can tell you all about that. That is why he comes and he goes, taking what scraps of employment might fall his way. He, unlike Tom Brett, has only himself to consider. A family man needs to be immune from the unpredictability that belongs with the precarious world of agriculture. This, above all, is what will draw him, along with dozens like him, away from village farms and into the industries that are springing up in the ever-growing market towns of Suffolk.

If he were to be really true to himself, Thomas Brett would in later years remember those early months of his marriage to Eleanor as the happiest of his life: when he was newly-wed and still tilling the soil. Within a year or two, he is to find it all comes resoundingly and shudderingly to an end.

The cramps, the flux, call it what you will: Eleanor feels ill for the first time. It is when Thomas would have been working on the harvest. But for a year now, he has worked at a maltings in Needham Market: a job he hates, but it enables him to be a better provider. To begin with, she takes to their bed. He is minded with caring for their son, who cries a good deal for his mother. There will be a lot of crying over the next days. Eleanor's mother comes to help. She makes up potions, but her sickening daughter cannot keep anything down. She passes blood, too much blood for it to be ignored. It is all so dreadfully fast. One day, she is playing with the baby. Two weeks later, exactly two and a half years from the date of their marriage, she is dead. Now how can that be?

Thomas Brett finds himself living alone with a year-old son in a house barely eight miles from where he was born, but it feels as if he is at the farthest end of the earth. One by one, his old friends from Stonham arrive to pay their respects. None was at his wedding and none at Eleanor's funeral. Slowly the word has reached them and slowly they will endeavour to bring him back into their world.

"Find a nurse for the child and ponder over where you go next." That is George's suggestion. 'Take your time', in other words.

"Get yourself out there and find another mother for that child." Sam Tricker offers that as his idea to alleviate the situation.

"Leave the boy with his gran'mother and get you back to work. Thass the best way." James Nunn's recommendation: very down-to-earth.

Then the master, Thomas Warren pays a visit. By now, Thomas has followed James Nunn's advice. He could not expect to hold on to his maltings cottage and remain away from work any longer. For the master it has been quite a journey from Debenham by horse and trap, but now he is here to offer his own message of counsel and consolation. His words are strange and Thomas is not sure quite what he means by them.

"I know how you are feeling. Just make sure that boy of yours isn't lost to you in all this. Keep him close and make your life around him, and it will come round right. It may not seem to be the most important thing right now, but whatever the future holds make sure you let him know he is the centre of your world."

All fine pieces of advice in their own way. All correct in their own way, and all followed by Tom Brett in his own way.

But it is Henry whose advice is what he most needs. Good old Henry who kept a watchful eye on him when he was the smallest in the class of '63. Henry Robinson, living the closest to Needham but the last of his friends to pay his respects turns up at Tom's door one evening, unannounced, unexpected.

"Get you back to Stonham bo'...," Henry says. "...where you got folks that care for you and a bit o' belonging."

He's right of course. He's given it his thought, and he can't understand why no-one else has come to the same conclusion. There are enough Bretts still in Stonham to raise another of their own kin while this child's father gets back to the only job he's ever felt at ease with. It won't mean an end to his sadness, but it will be a new beginning, flanked by familiarity.

For a short time, Thomas Brett wears his tragedy like a tattoo, though it will slowly fade. Over the first weeks after her death, his whole demeanour is of one in pain. Still, he has a son to consider, though he has to admit he never was much good at the mothering business. Not like George Buckle who can change and feed and rock babies to sleep; when he isn't working, that is. It is a good thing Tom lives among women with the knack of minding children. His mother and his sisters dote on the child.

On one occasion, he does take his boy to see the master. Not the most sensitive of men, he can't understand why Thomas and Martha Warren seem a little distant with him.

Chapter 17 ~ December 1781

"If John Coats by the age of twenty-one can see his way clear to paying off a debt, so should we all." That was the gist of George Buckle's speech four years earlier at the funeral.

It is all very well for George to make a statement like that, but of all the class of '63 he is one with the fewest pennies to rub together. He is the one with the commitments. Not that he'd have it any other way. Marrying Mary Nunn was the best thing he ever did. But four years on from the funeral and with children filling every inch of their tiny tied cottage, how is he ever to find ten pounds? Others have been more cautious. Thomas Brett waited for years to wed his Eleanor: for Isaac Pawsey it will take even longer. James Nunn is still courting, but not seriously, and no-one has seen Jerry Sharman for over a year, though word says he is doing alright for himself.

All this is hard for George who can't help but think of himself as the leader of the group. The eldest, the tallest and the loudest: that is how it has always been. But when he sees Isaac Pawsey strutting around the parish in his latest frock-coat and sporting a fashionable periwig, it is clear to George Buckle he has not made the same strides up the ladder to prosperity. And it hurts!

It is a time of great change. An exciting time. America has declared its independence. Soon France will rise up and throw over its Royalty. There is talk of war with Spain, with Holland: with half the world it seems. The opportunities are there for a true adventurer. George might have appeared the adventurer at the age of ten, but it is his step-brother William who went off in a ship to Canada and now fights the French in the First Battallion of Foot. Yet George, the one-time fortune-hunter who once thought to explore the world, dangles babies on his knee and harnesses horses for a precarious living just yards from the house where he was born. And he dreams of the day when a slice of luck should come his way.

Within the boundaries of Earl Stonham are four public Houses; that is to say, one inn and three beer-houses. Describing the Angel as an inn is a bit of an exaggeration. They can, at a pinch, accommodate travellers, but even they would admit they would struggle to offer comfortable board and lodging to any unwary traveller without a good deal of warning. So mostly, they are merely drinking rooms with, in some cases, the additional attraction of a skittle alley.

George Buckle does not frequent these places very often any more. He may be the one with the education, but his wife comes from Battisford and they know how to look after their pennies in Battisford. At least that is what she tells him when she relieves him of his earnings on a Friday night, giving him barely enough for a quart of ale to last the week. If the others from his class in school could see that, they would scarcely believe it. But he has to admit she is good at making his meagre earnings last, so he'll not complain. Huh! He wouldn't dare!

So it is he finds himself at the Shepherd and Dog one Saturday afternoon, more to prove to his friends that he isn't hen-pecked than for any other reason. Just into the only pint of the day, he, along with a handful of friends, hears a terrible kerfuffle outside in the yard. A horse has broken free from its tethers and is setting about kicking at walls and doors and anything that takes its fancy. Men are standing around unwilling to risk life and limb in pursuit of a lost cause. If the animal doesn't seriously harm itself it will be a miracle.

Now, George is good with horses. He knows how to handle them. It is what he does all day long. This one however looks a bit more temperamental than the Suffolks he is used to. 'But a horse is a horse,' thinks George, and because he is more concerned about the animal than the property it is fast demolishing he stands alongside the beast and lets it run out of some of its energy before taking hold of the reins and leading it, still kicking, across the road and down to Wix Green where he can give it a little more scope to dart this way and that before finally calming down. He has a carrot in his pocket. He always has these days. That is enough to endear him to any horse. He makes no attempt to mount the animal. That would be asking too much. And anyway, it would only be showing off.

Man and beast gently amble back to the scene of destruction. Cracknell is none too pleased with hoofmarks through his walls and doors. But grudgingly he says thanks, whilst adding that George might have been a bit quicker in getting the animal out of the yard.

However, it is the horse's owner who is more taken with this unassuming young man. His name is Nathaniel Studd and he keeps the Pye Coaching Inn beside the turnpike at Stonham Parva. For some reason, though nearly home, he has stopped off to moisten his palate. As a result of what he has just seen, he has an offer to make.

"I assume you work with horses?"

"Yes, sir. Every day. I look after them, harness them, coach them when they need coaching. I can even plough a fair straight furrow."

"I don't think you'll be needing to do that. But if you like to come and see me at the Magpye, we may be able to come to an arrangement."

And that is that. As luck would have it, the stabler at the Pye has just fallen foul of his master's displeasure once too often, leaving Mr Studd with the problem of changing up to twelve teams of horses a day, as well as preparing privately commissioned coaches and carriages. All on top of making sure the road-weary travellers are agreeably fed and vittled and, if necessary, bedded.

He needs a horseman - and quick!

Here, as if in answer to his prayer, is a young man deserving of a hefty increase in his weekly earnings: a modest drinker he is told, unlike the last one who was, like as not, to be found curled up in a pool of his own vomit, just when he was most needed.

After that, Nathaniel Studd discovers all those unknown qualities George has to recommend him. He can work under pressure, and there will be plenty of that. As well as the horses, he can manage the grooms and the stable boys, even though he is little older than most of them. Then, when Mr. Studd is considering rebuilding some of the stables and coach-houses, but cannot see his way clear to designing it all: why, George can draw him a plan that will demonstrate the most efficient lay-out. It seems too good to be true.

This all happens just at the time George and Mary Buckle find they are to be invited to attend Isaac Pawsey's wedding at Earl Stonham. Now he will have something to tell the rest of the group.

Quite a wedding it is too. Unfortunately, Isaac and his bride, Mary Martin have chosen a bitterly cold December day. Why then, nobody can understand. She doesn't even look pregnant. One or two of the guests are regretting dressing for fashion rather than the weather conditions. The Pawseys seem to have risen somewhat. Isaac and his brother now farm a piece of parish land. Though not exactly affluent, they no longer look like simple labourers and there is talk of Isaac becoming one of the village elite: an Overseer even.

Once again, Mr. Warren's boys find themselves reunited, this time together with the man himself. It is an opportunity to catch up on how things are progressing. Thomas Warren is ageing with an elegance and a sophistication he never had as a young man. Now turned fifty, his silver-grey hair makes him look more like

Martha’s father than her husband, but they seem content enough. They need to be. They work together, live together, do everything together, so it seems. Young Thomas, his son, is now a master wheelwright and has finally taken over the business from his grandfather. He and his father, sadly, have little to say to one another these days.

The schoolmaster has plenty to say to his old class - that class - the class of ’63, ’64 and half of ’65 for good measure. Once just frightened little boys. Now look at them. They speak as if they rule the world. James Nunn has finally grown, so it seems. He has filled out too, as have several of them. He is glad to see that Thomas Brett has brought a young lady with him. Already tired of mourning for Eleanor, he is just beginning to dip his feet into the water again, so to speak. Mind you, it doesn’t seem to have stopped him eyeing up the bridesmaids. Already, his new lady has noticed and has a face on her like curdled dough. It is not the first time. Thomas likes the ladies. That is all there is to it. But she’ll make him suffer later!

Most of the class are there. Only Jerry Sharman is missing. Nobody has heard from him for months. But that is how it is with him. It is nothing new. His comings and goings have always been a bit of a mystery.

As for Sam Tricker - now, surprises from Sam are never ending.

“I’ve got the chance of a shop,” he says suddenly, out of a rare moment of silence.

“What sort of shop? And what do you know about shop-keeping?” asks Henry Robinson.

“What is there to know? You buy stuff people want and you sell it to ’em at a bit more. Then you keep the profit.”

Enterprise and ambition. Now, who taught him that? It all sounds simple enough, but who among them would be prepared to try it? Samuel Tricker will. He has all the confidence in the world as far as his own abilities are concerned. He has learned about book-keeping, a good deal about trading corn and malt, and even got his head around the buying and renting of property. It hardly matters what he finally chooses to sell. The ways of the world are simple to his way of thinking. He has that manner about him. Yes, Sam Tricker will be alright.

As for the rest, they'll laugh and they'll mock amongst themselves, but secretly, they'll admire him, and when talking to others outside the group, he'll be held up as an example of all that an education can do for a boy.

Part

Two

Chapter 18 ~ 1771 and after

Education - now there's a word. Their schooling may only have lasted three years; less for some. But knowing they can do things that even their parents can't has endowed this little group with astonishing confidence. Take Henry Robinson for example.

He's known as Tich now - too many Henrys working there already. 'There' meaning a farm in Combs managed by his grandfather on his mother's side. The nickname 'Tich' was grandad's suggestion, and who is he to object, even if he does end up a head taller than most of them.

"You'll be Tich from now on. Get used to it," his grandad said the first day he arrived for work. The harvest was already in so, as chance would have it, he was given work with sheep and cattle - pigs too, sometimes. George may be good with horses but Henry - or Tich, that is - can work wonders with a cow with mastitis or a lame lamb. He's stronger now. That's what comes of being out in all weathers and working most days of every week; Sundays included. He knows how to milk a cow but doesn't have to any more. He supervises the milkmaids - that's a slice of luck: first crack at all the pretty virgins.

But as time passes and his value to his uncle increases, he has become less of a dalliance for them; more of a catch. One day, he might even be the farmer. Mr. Brown is his mother's father after all. That may give him an advantage, but there is more to it than that. He's special, is Tich. Unlike so many lads, he has not appeared to be in any great hurry, but only because he can identify the short-cuts. He writes things down. He has lists and plans and ways of organising his world. As others have noticed and oft-times commented, he is a young man on a mission. 'He'll not be easily distracted,' they say. What do they know?

He met Deborah when he was eighteen. She was fifteen and looked younger, which is probably why she was still available and unattached. And they knew immediately there was something special about the way they felt for one another. Maybe not love at first meeting, but quicker than he had thought possible. A miller's daughter, Debbie as he called her, was prettier than any milkmaid he'd ever seen. Auburn hair, down to her shoulders, the tightest of waists, not terribly shapely - she was too young at that stage. But he was drawn to her to the extent that he was prepared to abandon his philandering ways and wait for her to grow to love him as he felt he already loved her.

She in turn felt the first stirrings of desire whenever she was near Tich Robinson. Everything about him left her in no doubt he was the one for her. To begin with, opportunities were few. Her parents kept a strict eye on her. You could hardly blame them. They could see she was besotted and they'd seen all too often where that could lead.

For one wondrous summer she would occupy his every waking moment and colour his sleeping hours. He had gone to the mill with a sack of newly-threshed wheat at the time of year when it was just-spring. Much of the corn was threshed in the autumn but a small amount remained untouched. It made, his uncle used to say when he was living in Stonham, a stronger flour like that. Henry couldn't see why it should, but old William Robinson knew about things like that, and as Henry didn't have to bake it into bread himself, he couldn't really argue. Grandad Brown evidently believed it too, so there Henry found himself, on such an errand when from down the mill steps emerged this vision. 'Where have they been hiding her?' he asked himself. For in all the times he had been there, he had never caught sight of this lovely creature before. There was something almost faery about her. If she had turned to reveal a pair of wings attached to her, he'd not have been surprised.

After that, it was any excuse to visit the mill, and sometimes she was there, and sometimes she wasn't. But when she was, she was all smiles and paying him attention and not seeming to care that he smelt of the flock or that he was wretchedly dressed with uncombed hair most of the time. By the time the blackthorn blossom had given way to the may in the hedgerows they were walking out together. They did so much walking that summer, and he showed her what he knew of the countryside around - where to find plovers' eggs, or gather wool from the thorn bushes for spinning. He brought her gifts of wild flowers that looked like bees and tiny woodland strawberries.

Chastely, they kissed. It seemed almost wrong to him to expect more. Though the desire was there, it seemed unnecessary to alter what was almost perfect. And it would not have dawned on him now to seek comfort with anyone else. The milkmaids were not even a poor alternative.

"You know I like you...love you... a lot," she said one light evening in June. "But I'm not ready yet."

"I know," he replied.

"When I'm seventeen, then I'll be ready... if you can wait that long."

"Of course I can, so long as I can be with you, thass all I want."

"I know it's not easy, cos it in't easy for me, neither. And I know it certainly can't be easy for you." She knew. Of course she knew. All that kissing and pressing against one another. It was perfectly obvious how she made him feel.

"An' what with you bein' experienced with other gals..."

Now how was he meant to answer that? If she liked to think he was more knowledgeable, more adept than he really was, then let her. Really, his fumblings with farm lasses didn't amount to a lot when he thought about it. But he'd not felt like this about anyone before.

As the days grew longer towards midsummer, they found more chances to be alone, and with it to be a bit more daring.

"Hen't we bin terribly sinful?" she said, though they hadn't really; just enough to pretend to be.

Ever after, one day really stuck in his mind. It was a Sunday and after church they had wandered together, following paths and tracks deep into the Suffolk countryside, away from places and people. There was one particular footpath that followed the parish boundary. Henry had walked it once before at the beating of the bounds. This time it was different. Before, he had been part of a crowd. Now it was glorious. Hedges had greened to the extent that there were times when you could see little of the world the other side. Partridges flew up from the long grass underneath their feet. There were all kinds of birds singing that they couldn't put a name to. There were chiff-chaffs, of course, and wrens along the ditches as loud as they were tiny. Sheep in the streamside meadows were pushing away their growing lambs who were still trying to suckle. The high sky was almost kingfisher blue: the light hurt your eyes. There were just a few wisps of cloud. They'd thicken up later, but for that moment it couldn't have been more perfect. Looking back in later years, Henry would remember that day as the time when they were most together.

"Do you ever think you might like to go to a town?" she asked him.

"What, like Stowmarket or Framlingham?"

"No, bigger I mean; like Ipswich or Narwich or London."

"I wouldn't like it," he said. "Country's where I belong - you too I reckon."

"I went to Narwich once. Din't like it much. It smelt horrible," she confirmed.

"Well, there you are then."

They laughed. Then he stopped. He didn't want her to feel he was laughing at her.

"Oh I don't wanna stay there," she assured him, "just go, an' see."

He said nothing. He was still unconvinced.

When they had first started out together, they'd had so much to say. Now, there were long silences; instead, a lot of kissing and touching. At one point, stretched out across the path, concealed by the long grass, so absorbed in each other were they that they hardly noticed a lone walker who muttered as she stepped over them. Looking up, Debbie was relieved not to recognise her.

Barley ripened gold around them, the wheat still grey-green on the stalk. Swifts screamed above the clover. Cut hay shouted to be turned. You could smell the fresh lines of it ripening under the Sunday sky.

Such days were what he now lived for. All of which made Tich Robinson a bit of a liability around the farm. He'd always been so reliable. Now look at him, mooning about over some scrap of a girl! Forgetting to do half of what had been instructed. His grandad said as much. His grandma too. So they sat him down and talked a bit of sense into him.

"She's a pretty little thing, but she's very young - still got a lot of growing up to do. It in't fair on her and it certainly in't fair on you to expect at your ages to be tied one to t'other like this." That was grandad's advice.

"You need to let things cool a little. Come the harvest, there wun't be time to draw breath. And arter that there'll be time for cuddlin' a bit. In the meantime why don't you suggest the two-on-yer see a bit of other folks; give the both-on-yer a bit o' freedom." The way he said it, it almost made sense. It did make sense, especially as it was repeated a few times during the weeks leading up to and beyond haysel.

Life isn't very fair. Sometimes you meet the right person at the wrong time. The person with whom you are perfectly matched. But if the timing is wrong, however perfect the match, the moment slips away, and with it what might have been. The right person at the wrong time! Tragic: perhaps slightly less so than the alternative, but a sorry state of affairs nevertheless. And all because of some well-meant advice. That was when Henry Robinson learned that sometimes nothing is as toxic as the well-intentioned advice of others.

The summer came in a rush as it always did. Haymaking, then harvest. A little threshing and the start of ploughing the fields for winter. There was to be a good deal of celebrating what had been a well-planned operation and a fine harvest.

In all that time, Henry and Debbie saw very little of each other. As he said to her, "It's only fair that we should have the chance to be with other people, and as I'll not have a lot of time over the next weeks, we should be free to see other people if we want." She listened to his words, believing they were *his* words. It would not have occurred to her that in matters of the heart, he was almost as innocent as she. So she agreed with all he said. He in turn believed that this was a joint decision. Had they met a year or two later, neither would have given any credence to such a preposterous suggestion. They left it with the vague agreement that they would meet again at the harvest festival service at church 'after all was safely gathered in.'

In this way, the right people meeting at the wrong time made the first of some rather unfortunate decisions. It didn't seem so bad then. It would pass. Harvest would come to an end and then they'd see one another once more. Henry, after days in the harvest fields, supped with the rest and after a few pints and quarts of ale found solace with several lasses more than willing to help him forget his faery girl.

Then a note arrived. It was from Debbie. That in itself came as a bit of a surprise. To his knowledge, whilst she could read a bit, she had never been taught to write. Someone else had penned these most intimate of lines.

'I am sorry,' the letter began, 'but I cannot see you no more. Something has happened, and we cannot be together no more. You can't come here. I am sorry.'
'What,' he wondered, 'did that mean?' There was nothing more in the note. That was all. It was over. Finished. He was not to go there.

But of course he did. Those words struck him like a thunderbolt. All the time he had been cropping corn, tying up sheaves, sharpening scythes; all the time he had been supping ale and nuzzling up to labourers' daughters; all the time he had been following the suggestions of others, it had not so much as entered his mind that Debbie might have been doing precisely what he had suggested she should.

Mounting his grandfather's favourite horse, he rode...no, he galloped towards the mill cottage. Had he worn spurs, he would have spurred his way down what amounted to a highway. But though he knocked and called aloud, she would not see him. He never did hear the full details of the matter. Clearly she had met someone. Added to which she had received information regarding his own peccadilloes. It had all gone further than she had intended. Further than she had with him. And somehow she couldn't get it out of her head that it was his fault. Now why was that?

The right person at the wrong time.

There were to be long moments of self recrimination. Then the blaming of everybody but himself. From others came familiar platitudes - plenty more fish in the sea - and all that, but when you have sampled turbot, knowing sardines are on offer doesn't really help. It would be comforting to believe it all came right in the end. But no, the moment was past, leaving a regret that even with the passing of time and all the pleasures to follow, never entirely went away.

This is why, when he met again with his old schoolfriends at John Coats' funeral, and cast an eye over those now comfortably partnered, he still felt a shudder of the desolation he had suffered all of five years before, knowing his loss hadn't and wouldn't ever leave him.

Chapter 19 ~ 1784

Within a year of being widowed, Tom is once more in love; at least, he says he is. Tom Brett, being Tom Brett has a lot to say about love.

"I only bin in love six times this week. I got ill on Wednesday."

"Every man want a woman what look like the Virgin Mary, cook like his ol' grandmother, is as faithful as his dog and join giblets like the jug-girl down the Angel." This last offering is accompanied by the rapid upward movement of a clenched right fist (It might be any jug-girl from the Angel - the publican there has a penchant for pretty girls, as everybody knows).

"But," he continues sadly, "We usually end up with a woman what look like your ol' grandmother, cook like your dog, is as faithful as the jug-girl from the Angel, an' bury the beef like the Virgin Mary."

At which point, the beerhouse owner may feel it necessary to remind him to watch his language. As has been added, "There might be ladies present." Though when a lady was last seen in the tap room of the Shepherd and Dog, no-one can remember.

"In Stonham we make the distinction between them gals what you takes into a church and them what you takes into a cornfield."

That's a favourite of his: usually after a drink or three. Now it seems he has found another girl who fits into the former group.

The problem is, she - Rachel Green, that is - seems rather reluctant to marry him. She will live with him, bear his children even, but she wants to find out what kind of husband he will make before she decides to walk up the aisle with him. So Thomas Brett is on his best behaviour, and has been for some time.

All of this comes as something of a surprise to his friends

who would normally be cautious of allowing their wives and lady-friends to get too close to philandering Thomas. And they all have their own attitudes regarding the situation.

"She'll do. She's presentable and she keeps him in order." Samuel Tricker's words. Not exactly how James Nunn would word it but similar in sentiment.

"Of course they should be married - it's not decent to be otherwise," says Isaac Pawsey of all people. Now when did he start to be so right and proper?

As far as Henry Robinson is concerned, love is all that matters and everything else is just detail.

As for George Buckle, surrounded by children, he is too wrapped up in his own family affairs even to present an opinion.

Tom and Rachel meet at the Cherry Fair in Stowmarket. It is not that he is actually looking for a partner when he travels into town that day. Like so much in his life it just happens to him, unplanned, unpredicted, unexpected. A wink, a dance, a promise to meet again, and look where it gets you!

Where it gets them both is no place to be for a few stolen hours a week. Not that that seems to stop them. Days together may mean travelling the four miles between their homes and seeking seclusion, but all it demands is creativity to match the desire. There proves to be no shortage of either and before they know it, as the old song goes, her apron strings no longer tie.

For some time, Rachel has been in service, minding the children of those who can afford the luxury of a nursemaid. Fortunately she is highly regarded by her employers, the Marriotts of Thorney Hall. Even when she informs them she is to have a child of her own, they have no wish to lose her. Sorry to part with such a treasure, they continue to accept her into their house until her size renders it impossible. Now they have promised to find her a position should she ever wish to return. By that, they mean should her infant, like so many others, fail to survive.

The Bretts are no strangers to bastards in the family and have proved remarkably tolerant about the whole business. Rachel's family are living forty miles away, so as first one, then a second daughter appears, everyone becomes resigned to the way things are. Such is life in Earl Stonham.

But a marriage there will be. Again, it is a muted affair back in Rachel's home parish in Norwich. Now with two of her own children and an adopted one from Tom's first marriage, Rachel has permanently left her position as nursemaid and devotes her time to her own growing clutch.

Once more, it is a struggle to feed and clothe a family. It's fine when harvest brings bonuses to those willing to work long hours. But as each winter draws to a close, pickings are thin and lay-offs inevitable. The Bretts gravitate back towards town where work doesn't disappear at the first sign of bad weather. It was not a choice he made gladly before, and each time necessity makes it harder.

This time, it is to Stowmarket, they move. Sam Tricker helps him find a small cottage at an affordable rent. Here they will forge a different life; different work; different friends; different pastimes; but the same old problems.

*　　　　*　　　　*　　　　*　　　　*

It was never actually an apprenticeship - not really - not the signed indenture with money changing hands kind of apprenticeship. Not at all. James Nunn may have been led to believe it was. Or he may just have told it like that to his friends and even the schoolmaster. Truth to tell, it was an arrangement whereby the lad would do a great deal of pumping bellows whilst picking up smatterings of old Tye's smithing technique. At times, he hardly knew how to stand: every limb ached; but that wasn't going to get in his way. He would sleep beside the smith's anvil and be fed left-overs, for which he was meant to be audibly grateful. He even put up with that.

There were doubts over whether Sonny Tye was a real blacksmith at all, but he had worked a forge at Brockford for enough years to have found out a thing or two. He got through bellow-boys at the rate of about four a year - before James Nunn came, that is. Perhaps surprisingly, this lad stayed. Not just the customary few months, but a year turned into half a dozen and before you knew it, other boys were pumping the bellows and he was doing some tinkering work of his own. Folks soon got to know that here was place that you could get things repaired - pots and pans long past their best, but still capable of giving a few years' service.

Sonny Tye still did the 'skilled work' as he described it, but he soon recognised his young 'apprentice' was remarkably adept at creating tools of his own design and before you knew it, people were beating a path to his door in search of items they never knew existed. An adjustable wheeled hoe that ran between the rows and took out the weeds; a ploughshare that could be made to attach to any plough that could be angled to plough at different depths in different years; a cooking pot with sections to enable the cooking of several separate items at once. There seemed no end to this boy's creativity. And when word reached Thomas Warren his old schoolmaster some time later, he would smile and remember the small boy whom he had encouraged to draw and to make things.

So many things in life are life-threatening. It has been stated before, but it is worth re-iterating. The world is a dangerous place. The world of work even more so!

How many have waved goodbye in the morning to a husband, wife or child, never to greet them home at day's end? And few occupations are more prone to fatality than work on a farm. It is hard to say how many of Earl Stonham's five hundred souls are employed on its twenty farms and smallholdings -

probably most of them: and the majority probably rarely give a thought to the dangers they might encounter daily.

The evidence is there for all to know through the Coroner's inquisitions reported in newspapers and by word of mouth. There was John Brundish over at Framsden, shifting a tumbril of hay when the horse balked and he and the load shifted. He ended with a pitchfork through his belly and died a day later. There was Minnie Moyes, hit by a windmill sail. 'Just careless', the Coroner said. Manny Mitchell went out in the morning to dig a well: he never came home; the clay had caved in and buried him. Puch Taylor was kicked by a mare and never came to. Then Mary Larter died over at Framlingham - her employers found her dead in a field - they never worked out what killed her - lightning, somebody suggested. No, you don't need to be a soldier or a fisherman to be doing a dangerous job.

Then there are accidents on the road. It is never easy handling horses and waggons. The roads are mostly rutted and uneven. It isn't too bad on the flat, but get a heavy load up and a slope to negotiate and it is the recipe for disaster. Some people laugh and say there aren't any hills in Suffolk, but carriers and coachmen know different. The hill down from Forward Green to the house at Halefield just above the church in Earl Stonham is a case in question. So too is taking loads up in either direction along the turnpike from the crossroads by the Brewery Tap. Going uphill is perilous; downhill worse. Horses are all too often called upon to pull loads that are heavy enough on the level, but way beyond their limited horse-power on even the smallest incline. So it is that accidents happen.

Tom Baldwin, Prim Peck, Joe Markham: all local men who died within a few months of one another; and for a while employers made an effort to provide their drivers with horses enough for the task in hand. Then Eddie Welham went under the wheels of the waggon he was driving, having fallen from the shafts he was sitting on. 'Too much drink', they said. But once again it was a loss of control by horse and driver when faced by a steep hill. What was needed when going uphill, someone suggested was a brake that would hold the vehicle once the horses had run out of momentum. Then they could have a breather whilst re-gathering the energy to continue.

Similarly, a brake was needed to prevent the vehicle careering away with horse and driver, allowing a more sedate and safe descent. That is where James Nunn comes in. It is one thing tinkering and playing at inventing things, but this is an altogether more serious matter. Towards the end of March 1784, two strangers arrive at the Brockford forge with an idea for him to consider.

The taller of the two is a carrier from Felsham by the name of Boggis, testament to just how far James Nunn's reputation has spread. The other is a farmer from Nedging, somewhat appropriately called Clover. Mr Clover it seems lives close to a particularly dangerous hill on which accidents are not infrequent. The two have been seeking an answer to the problem for some time. Hearing of this inventive young man, they have made the not inconsiderable journey to hear what he might have to offer.

"We have tried braking systems on our carts and waggons," says Boggis, "But as soon as any great weight is carried, they don't b'luddy work. Even the drivers of the mail coaches have this problem, which is why they get riled if you ask 'em carry more than they have to."

"The way I see it," continues Clover, "Whatever you make the brakes from, more weight makes the wheels slip and get hot and then they slip all the more."

"Have you tried iron?" asks old man Tye, ever the blacksmith. "I find iron does right well for most things."

"People have been trying iron and wood and leather and bone for as long as I remember and it still comes down to the fact that Semer Hill is a positive graveyard for wheeled transport and its drivers; not to mention the poor ol' horses."

"Then perhaps what you are looking for is a brake that pushes on the road rather than the wheels."

At this, eyes are suddenly all trained on James Nunn.

"I would need to see and measure the vehicle we intend to work on first. But I see no reason why it shouldn't be possible to make even Semer Hill a safer place."

Then, as if he has been working this out in his mind for some time, he picks up a piece of chalk and sketches out on a bench the image, not only of the brake, but the waggon, the driver and horses, all with such virtuosity and artistry, it completely silences the onlookers.

It isn't an entirely original idea. It has been tried before. Surveyors responsible for the upkeep of roads passing through their parishes detest anything that might gauge holes in the highways. But as far as James Nunn is concerned, lives saved are more important than a few holes to be filled in. Anxious to avoid trouble with the authorities, his brake is designed to cause the minimum of damage, though the Turnpike Trust will need more convincing. They have already legislated against waggons with the narrowest of wheels. Now James Nunn's new brake threatens to wreak havok on their precious road surface. Fortunately, they are a little slow in reacting to what is happening in central Suffolk. By the time their objections are being voiced, he can show how much safer he has made the roads. Of the waggons and coaches using his system, only two have suffered serious accidents on slopes and inclines. Not a single death has occurred in that time.

On the strength of all this, he will never be a truly rich man, but will eventually see his way clear to regard himself less a smith and more an engineer. The money he makes will buy him a small cottage in Mendlesham. And eventually he'll even find time in all this to go courting.

The first time he had met Mary Howes, to be honest, she had not made a great impression on him. Likewise, this man with permanently filthy face and hands had not appealed much to her. Wetheringsett is an oddly scattered village - two, maybe three hamlets really, a mile or so separating each. Mary lived in the main village, a mile or two away from Brockford Forge and close to the church and the White Horse. Her parents kept a few assorted animals and had sent their daughter once in a while to the village forge to have metal items made or repaired.

She had returned one day in tears complaining of the treatment she had received from Posy Hood. A man of few words and wandering hands, he was notorious and Mary Howes' father should have known better than to expect any different.

His first inclination was to 'sort it out' with the smith, which would not have been an awfully good idea, bearing in mind the respective sizes of the two potential combatants. Instead, Gully Howes was persuaded to hit the local smith the way it would hurt him most - in his pocket, by transferring all his business to the smithy down the road at Brockford. Added to which, he recommended all of his many friends did the same.

By this time, Sonny Tye tended to leave most of the work to James Nunn, preferring to occupy a bench in the Griffin most days, after which it seemed generally safer not to have him playing with or anywhere near fire.

Timid Mary Howes has for a while been visiting the forge in what is only to be described as a business capacity. Throughout this, she has been unable or unwilling to be in any way other than business-like. Which is why it comes as a bit of a surprise to both she and the young smith to discover they are starting to enjoy the occasional discourse accompanying the shoeing of a pony or the forging of a chain.

Then...

"They say, you're being a bit of an inventor."

"Do they now? And who might 'they' be?"

He is teasing her. But she doesn't mind. In fact, she quite likes it. "My dad - he say you made coaches stop crashin'."

"Well, I can't take all the credit for that. I just attached bits of metal that stopped waggons and the like from running away," he explains. "Mind you, I can't stop some fool of a driver from stopping off at the Magpye and drinking himself stupid before trying to rattle down Stonham Hill with him sitting astride the shafts with the reins round his neck."

She giggles, only to have this serious young man snap back, "Thass alright for you to laugh, but you hen't had the job of clearin' the bits up arter an acciden' like that. 'Tin't pretty I can tell yer."

No she hasn't, but if truth be told, neither has he. Still he feels he ought to put this frivolous young girl in her place, even if he is beginning to quite take a fancy to her.

As for Mary Howes, she knows full well there is no way she is going to be lectured to by a grubby smith. Her answer is to make sure she doesn't come back for at least a fortnight. Not that he seems to have noticed.

When she finally does return, he behaves as if nothing unpleasant has passed between them, or that she has taken leave of his establishment for any longer than might be expected.

On another occasion she struggles to unload a heavy coffer with broken hinges. He makes no effort to help; merely smiling and beating his hammer on a piece of iron that really needs no working other than to give the appearance of being busy. Then, when she finally has manoeuvred it into a position to be seen, he idly remarks, "Oh, you should have asked me to give you a hand with that." As if she would deign to ask him for anything!

Then, to add insult to injury, he forges and attaches new hinges before whisking the finished article up above his head and aboard her carriage as if it was as light as thistledown (and what was all the fuss about?).

Eventually, it occurs to the two of them that they irritate each other so much they must be in love and maybe they might like to walk out together. Then follows a lengthy period of squabbles and disagreements, break-ups and back-togethers until the two of them and their families despair of anything coming of it at all. They can't be together and they can't be apart. They seem to delight in winding one another up like watch-springs. Better mannered wars have been fought than their courtship.

Conversations with friends tend to begin, "Do you know what that woman said?" or "I'll have nothing more to do with that arrogant so and so!"

And so it goes on for so long until finally their friends say, "For the Lord's sake, you can't bear to be apart so you'd better be together." Even then it takes till 1793 for the two of them to agree to wed in Wetheringsett church. Not that anyone believes it will put an end to all their bickering.

Chapter 20 ~ March 1793

Thomas and Rachel Brett come to the wedding. It might have been better if they hadn't. They bring with them an atmosphere of malice and resentment that threatens to engulf the event. You can't ignore it. It takes the form of a black tide of despondency and despair just waiting to burst forth and swamp anyone close enough to be caught in its wake. An ill-chosen word, even the wrong kind of look, and they must have known whatever it was would become as public as a town-crier's announcement. Of course, it had to be George who would put his big foot right in it.

Fortunately, the Bretts are not the only quarrelsome ones there. No, the 'happy couple' are perfectly capable of making the merriest occasion mournful. They disagree on everything as a matter of course. They always do. It is nothing new. But right now, the Bretts are the focus of attention. They haven't spoken a word to one another, civil or otherwise, since they've arrived, and it hasn't gone without notice.

"Wass 'e bin up to this time?"

"Where's he bin dippin' it now?"

Such comments are frequently bandied around, often without much foundation, but this time there is more truth there than they realise.

They have all been invited; the class of '63 as they now refer to themselves. The bride cannot understand why. Haven't they both got more than enough relatives to fill the White Horse three times over? But true to form this will be an argument set to run and run. In the end, James Nunn has had his way. There is even an empty chair at the reception for the one of the class who can't be there, John Coats. Now that, Mary says, is just downright weird. An empty place at table like King Arthur's *siege perilous*. Where is the sense in that? But James has put his foot down and this time there is no chance of his giving way.

Meanwhile Thomas Brett is renewing acquaintances with those he's not seen in a while. Thomas Warren, the master, is there, sprightly as ever, but somehow shrunk from his memory. Still the schoolmaster at the Sir Robert Hitcham School in the centre of Debenham, he has aged gently and no longer looks like his wife's father. She in turn has filled out considerably, evidence of contentment and good living.

But it is clear to all that Tom Brett's mind is far from at ease in the company with whom he should have been easiest. There has been a summons. He'd been expecting it, but now it has arrived, publicly demonstrating his most singular weakness. Some men drink. Others gamble. He's done both in his time, though never to excess. But he does like the women, does Thomas Brett. Rachel knew when she married him he had a roving eye, but of course she thought he'd change. Or more to the point, she had thought she would change him. Now, pushing past the middle of life, and a family man at that, he is still at it.

Just before they had left home for the wedding, the court summons had arrived. Though it was beyond her limited reading ability to make sense of the words, she'd seen such documents before and she knew only too well that they always mean trouble.

In the end, she had wheedled it out of him. A recognition of bastardy, they called it. Susan Subtle of all people. Her best friend! Huh! Not any more she in't. And how is he meant to support another woman's child when he can barely support his own? No wonder the pair of them have arrived in a less than celebratory mood.

Thomas is glad to escape her sullen scowls and meet old friends. However, he thinks it wise to keep his guilty secret to himself for the time being. He knows he has transgressed, even by his standards, and he's not too proud of it.

Yes, they are all there; those still alive. Even Jerry Sharman. At first, nobody recognised him. Heavily bearded, birds-nest for hair, clothes that have seen better days. He was hiding, so it appeared, in a corner of the room. He had been at the back of the church throughout the wedding, so no-one had seen him.

"Is that Jerry?" asks Henry Robinson, he being the only other one of the group to be there on his own. Relationships never seem to last with him these days, and he has nobody to ask to come with him.

"Good Lord, it whully is," says George Buckle, darting across the room to say hello to his old friend.

Truth to tell, the man who had been baptised Jacob but was always known to his friends as Jerry is pleased to see they do not appear to despise him for his obvious continual brushes with poverty.

"Where have you been? Why didn't you write to any of us? Even the master say he's not heard from you." An assortment of questions as the old class crowd around their colleague. Even Thomas Warren has now gravitated to that corner of the White Horse.

Jerry Sharman tries to stand tall, but he's all too aware that those around him, his old classmates of thirty years earlier, look so much more affluent; more established; more confident.

"I do alright, though it in't always easy. Folks don' allers unnerstan' 'bout the Friends." By this, he means the Quakers. It has never been easy. "Folks don' trust us. Wun't give us employmen'. Can't lease land cos they want us to pay tithes. We don' pay tithes to a church we don' believe in. 'Tin't easy. 'Tin't easy."

For George Buckle, to whom decisions in life are always straightforward and simple, this makes no sense at all.

"Jus' don' tell'em. What folks don' know won't hurt 'em. An' as for tithes, well, nobody pays half what they oughter: you jus' lie about it, I s'pose."

It is plain to everyone else that is no sort of answer, but it is George's way of looking at the world and it serves him.

Altogether more thoughtful and quieter, Sam Tricker and his wife Mary stand back and consider. "Can't you do something?" she whispers.

"I might. Jus' give me a while." And he sinks into thought and reflection whilst others talk several legs off a number of proverbial donkeys.

When he does finally speak to his old classmate, it is as vague as to say, "I may have a place for you; if you can bear to leave workin' the land. Jus' ask folk in Stow: they'll tell you where we live. Everyone know Sam Tricker."

With that much done, Sam rejoins his wife at the edge of the throng.

That is when George sticks his hobnail right in it. For once, Rachel Brett has found her way to her husband's side and even appears vaguely affectionate. In truth, she wants to keep a watchful eye on Thomas. There aren't a number of great beauties in attendance as far as she can see, but as Thomas has aged, he has become a little less fussy. If ask her about his preferences, she would probably answer, "Anything female, sixteen to sixty: with Thomas you never can tell."

"Well, George, any more littl'uns on the way?" That is Henry. They all find George's burgeoning brood a source of great amusement.

"Do yew know - we gone two years since the last and it in't cos I gorn off 'er," laughs George. "Isaac's found the answer - jus' two pretty little ol' gals. I'd like to know how he planned that one. You could sell it if you knew the secret." They all, laugh, Isaac included.

"Of course, some onnus left it a bit late," carries on George looking first at Sam Tricker and then at the new bridegroom.

"We go for quality, not quantity, snaps back Sam.

Like so much in Samuel Tricker's life, marriage has been a practical and ordered decision. Mary Pyman, daughter of a Stowupland shopkeeper must have felt her time had passed when romance would present itself. She was pleasant enough; just rather unexciting, preferring to balance her father's books than go dancing, for example. That was what attracted her to Samuel Tricker. Not the world's greatest romantic himself, he wanted a partner who would share his interest in business, and play an equal part in his future success. He supposes he loves her, and she him, and maybe they do. But at least they have a lot in common.

That is when George turns his attention to Tom Brett. It is only a joke; a bit of ribaldry, that's all. "An' what about you Thomas? Got any more little Bretts about to hatch? Might some-one be farrowin' down agin soon?"

Oh dear, if he had only known. But how was he to? And it is all meant in the best of spirits. Little is he to know what a furore he is about to spark. George and his big mouth!

"Little Bretts - You ask 'im," yells Rachel at the top of her considerable voice. "Little f'ckin' Bretts! Who knows how many little f'ckin' Bretts there are. Ask Susan Subtle. Ask anyone else that's carrying his bastards. Well there un't gonna be no more little f'ckin' Bretts from this body. Not that there'll be any short-age of little f'ckin' Bretts. Cos he don't know how to stop fillin' the world with little f'ckin' Bretts." At which point, she dissolves into tears and the ministrations of the other wives.

"Oh dear George," remarks Henry, "why is it allers you?"

George is flustering, "What did I do?"

Thomas just puts his hand on his friend's shoulder. "Don't take it to heart. If it hadn't a-bin you, it would a-bin someone. It was jus' waitin' to come out."

Mary Tricker isn't the only one muttering to herself, "Did she just say what I thought she said?"

A picture of innocence: the newly married Mrs. Nunn is quite shocked. She has never heard a woman swear before. Thomas Warren sits thinking to himself, "Thank goodness I only had boys in that class."

A short while later, Mary Buckle finds herself talking to the old schoolmaster. For once, he is on his own. His wife has drifted off to chat to another one of her endless relatives. The boys have all been talking together across the other side of the room for some time. She knows Thomas Warren well. George has made sure of that.

"Do you see much of your Thomas and Elizabeth?" she asks.

"To tell you the truth, they've not spent much time with me since their mother died. I think it was probably for the best that I moved away. Now they are grown up and have their own lives to lead. Thomas is doing well as a wheelwright. He's marrying soon: at Wetheringsett. So's Elizabeth."

"What's her man like - Do you find him agreeable?" she asks, but the schoolmaster shakes his head sadly. "I've never met him. I don't expect an invitation."

Then, perking up, he says, "Never mind me, how about your brood. They must be growing fast. Where are they?"

"I 'spec' you can hear 'em," Mary replies. "They're usually the loudest. There are clear shrieks echoing from outside. The children are having no problem entertaining themselves.

"They can read a bit," she said. "George is learning 'em."

Ever the teacher, Thomas Warren has to stifle the urge to correct her.

"Our eldest, George he did go to be taught at the school by Mr. Pizzey, but he in't so good as you. His dad do it now. He do say he can't help much but he can give 'em the rudi..ments I think he say. I don't know where he get these words - read 'em I s'pose. Sounds rude to me. But then girls don't get to read usually, do they?"

"They do in my school."

"No?"

"Indeed. In Debenham we now have girls learning to read and to write, though accounts we leave to the boys. Their heads are better designed to understand numbers."

To Mary Buckle it is almost magical to believe that girls might attend school and learn the way her George had done all those years ago.

As the warring couple prepares to leave, George, ever-apologetic, mutters simply, "What'll you do now?"

"I dunno," says Tom, "Say sorry a lot, I s'pose..."

He pauses to shrug a shoulder. "I'm good at that. I had a lotta practice."

The reception begins to break up slowly. It isn't so much that Rachel Brett's outburst has soured the occasion - for some, it has been the highlight of the day and will offer a talking point for a while to come - but with Thomas and Rachel Brett leaving, the class of '63 is no longer complete, so there is no point in being there any longer.

"I'd say he married the wrong gal," says Sam Tricker.

"Wass wrong with Rachel?" asks Mary Nunn, still in her bridal attire.

"Wrong name - hen't you noticed? We all married Marys, like most of our mothers. Now there's a good solid name is Mary." That is the closest thing to a joke you are likely to hear from Sam Tricker.

As for Henry Robinson, he is only too glad of an excuse to leave. So many others are comfortably partnered. Even the less comfortable partnerships seem better than none at all. Oh, he isn't the only one; he knows that. There is Jerry Sharman, but somehow even though he appears to have fallen on hard times, he seems complete as if his own company is enough for him. Whereas Henry feels like 'poor old Henry.' He can only imagine what will be said after he leaves.

At the other side of the room, Jerry Sharman is also attempting to depart unnoticed. Mary Tricker catches him edging out of the door.

"He meant it you know - we both did... do. Speak to him... when you're ready." She hardly suspects he will.

Chapter 21 ~ April 1793

Sam and Mary Tricker have it all. That is how they see it. They manage two shops in town, added to which they deal in all manner of commodities. What a partnership! Tom Brett laughingly refers to them as 'Tricker and Tricker incorporated'. Their work is their work, but also their play, their focus, their recreation. They are of one mind, one intention, one determination and, just occasionally, one body. As a result a small family has brought about an expansion of their once meagre accommodation above the shop in Bury Street.

Not for them the grand house and the trappings of wealth and success. Such as they now own has come too easily by their way of thinking to be confident it can't be snatched away by the vagaries of luck or misfortune. They have both grown up in homes far meaner than this and crave no more than they now possess.

Their children might spend much of their childhood under the gaze and protection of others whilst their parents barter and sell whatever turns a profit. But they too will learn their parents' work-ethic and, in time, find their own delight in commerce.

Jerry Sharman comes calling just two weeks after the wedding. He has found it simple enough to find his old class-mate's home. The Trickers are well-known in and around Stowmarket. It is a good thing they are. Neither of the shops they own bears their name at this time: that will have to wait another generation. They are content instead to trade under names that carry the good-will of decades.

When the door is opened to him, Mary Tricker is relieved to see that he's tidied himself up a little.

"You did say, you might have something for me," he begins.

"And you did say it was genuinely meant." He is unsure which of the pair he should be addressing.

"You still remember how to read and write?"

"I can read the Bible and copy out verses."

"What I meant... that is to say *we* meant... is that through our family and other connections, there are places for people who can keep accounts, logs and records of dealings. I seem to remember you were the best of us... back then." When Sam Tricker speaks, it is clear he is speaking for the two of them.

"Here in town I have an uncle who is a cooper," he continues. "He makes a good barrel but is criminally lax when it comes to chasing those who owe him money. In a similar way my brother-in-law runs the family store in Stowupland just across the river. He is a good salesman, but a terrible business man. There are other ventures we have in mind, especially in the villages around. Tom Brett's eldest is to 'prentice as a baker in Mendlesham. The old baker is approaching retiring, and has no son to take on the business. Just another of our little undertakings, Mary and me. Where we can, we help our friends. And it bothers us not which church they choose to attend. We are dissenters ourselves these days. We have much in common with your good self."

"I don't know what to say," Jerry Sharman shuffles his feet awkwardly.

"As I said. Those used to long days in the open air may miss its allure." He stops a moment, almost embarrassed to sound quite so poetic.

"No, there was never a lot of allure diggin' out ditches in the worst of what winter had to throw at you. An' hoein' for hours, or liftin' taters or mangles. No, I can do without that sort of allure. An' the wages poor an' every chance if there was no work, you'd be laid off unless proper contracted."

"You take to this work and there'll be no layin' off for bad weather. An' it will be paid better than labourin' - not a lot, but steady like."

The arrangement is that he will be accommodated for the time being in a room adjoining the Coopers business in Violet Hill. Never a man to give way to excitement, for once Jerry Sharman feels like celebrating. Being teetotal, a cup of small ale will have to suffice. After that he intends to give his life and a portion of his soul to the task, to prove Sam's faith in him has not been misplaced. His first major success will be to contract Old Tricker to construct a hundred barrels for a brewery in Ipswich.

"An' how we gonna get them there?" asks the old man. "Float 'em down the river?"

"Very nearly," grins Jerry. He likes the old chap immensely. "You make 'em: I'll see they gets there."

And he does. With a team of boys to roll the barrels downhill from the works to the Navigation Wharf early in the morning, they are loaded aboard horse-drawn barges to travel the length of the new navigation from Stowmarket to Ipswich. The complete consignment arrives safely the same day having passed through fifteen locks on the way. It seems almost magical.

The wedding at Mendlesham turns out to be the last time that the remaining seven of what had been eight: the class of '63, will all meet together. There have been promises to meet up somewhere at some unstated date, but as time has moved on, it just seems like it wasn't to be. Good intentions aren't enough in themselves, and those with the power to have made it happen are too busy getting on with their own lives.

Instead they have to settle for meeting up in twos and threes. Only Isaac Pawsey now lives in Earl Stonham, and it is left to him to make the best he can of passing the news from Henry, Jerry, Thomas and Sam living around Stowmarket to George and James out in 'those rum owd places', as he refers to them.

George and James will, once a month, make the short journey to Debenham to visit the master. In the news that continues to be passed between them, Tom Brett, Henry Robinson and Jerry Sharman in particular continue to feature, looming large in the order of things.

Chapter 22 ~ 1798

The door of Tom and Rachel Brett's house has never had a knocker. Most times, it has no need of one. People tap and walk in. But one day in late September, someone hammers hard on the door and waits. Rachel Brett is preparing a meal in the hope her husband might deign to put in an appearance. No, to be honest, since the Nunns' wedding, he has hardly put a foot wrong. Which is why it is such a surprise to see who is standing at the door.

"What do *you* want?" she snaps.

"Can I just come in a minute?" asks Susan Subtle.

"I don't think I want you here."

"Please," Susan says, revealing the small child who has been hiding behind her.

"Well, there's no doubtin' who that 'un belongs to. Looks jus' like all of mine." The small boy smiles at her.

"Oh well, I s'pose you better come in."

Susan Subtle: now who would have believed she'd dare show her face? Admittedly, she only lives up the road and around the corner, but it must have been five years since they have passed a civil word together. Every week, she has presented ninepence of their hard-earned money to the Overseers to ensure the mother of her husband's bastard has been cared for. It doesn't make for an easy reconciliation. But they were once close and now that two of her own children are offhand, Rachel finds it is quite nice to have another small child around the house, even if he is as timid as a church mouse.

"I s'pose you'd like a cup of tea?" Of course she would. She can't often afford tea, not even cut-price smugglers' tea such as is on offer here.

"There is a reason why I've come," she says.

"I thought there might be - go on."

"It might be good news as far as you'd be concerned. I'm gettin' married."

Now that is a surprise. Not every man wants someone else's child to bring up.

"Where did you meet?" asked Rachel.

"He was on manoeuvres nearby. He stopped to talk to me and we got on right well. He loves this little'un. We're gettin' wed in three weeks time, once the banns are called - in Colchester."

"He's a soldier then?"

"Yes, but not like your usual soldier. More refined. He's a corporal. He can read and write, jus' like your Thomas."

There has to be more to it than this. Rachel waits for the next piece of information to present itself.

"He want to adopt Tommy." Then to clarify matters, Susan says, "I called him Tommy." She waits a moment for this to sink in before announcing, "So you won't need to pay me no more, cos he wun't be your responsibility." The last word is pronounced with some difficulty.

That, as chance would have it, is the moment when Tom Brett choses to make his dramatic entrance. Spotting mother and child in his front room, "Oh shit!" he says.

"No Tom, it's alright. Susan has come to bring us some news... some very good news." She then explains the reason for Susan Subtle's visit. His reaction is not what she or Susan might have expected. Tears come into his eyes and he stammers, "So I don't get to be his dad no more?"

"You haven't really been much of a dad to him since he was conceived. So don't give me that ol' squit," snaps Susan.

"Hen't I,? Then why am I late home from work whenever I think I might pass your house in the hope of seein' him playin'. You know who I am, don't you, Tommy boy?" he says and to the surprise of the two women, the boy nuzzles up to him as though it were the most natural meeting of father and son.

"You mean when he come in with little treats, thass where he gets'em?" says Susan.

"Of course, you don't think I'd ignore my own son for five years?" The tears are really moistening his eyes now and the child looks concerned.

"Susan, you take the boy home. We'll talk this over. Come and see me another day, right."

That night there is some long hard talking. Thomas is quite reluctant to hand the welfare of his boy to an unknown soldier. But Rachel is more hard-headed and can see the advantage of no longer having to pay that money over each week. Also, occasional treats are one thing, but that is not what being a father is about. She lays this on with the proverbial trowel. He has to admit she has a point. He'll miss coming the long way home in hope of catching a sight of his boy, but he still has two children at home to fuss over. In the end, reluctantly, he has to agree, though just to make sure, Rachel has one more weapon in her armoury

"You know that ol' Bible what you got at school all them years ago - how you never thought you'd do what John Coats done - save up ten pounds. We've been payin' Susan's ninepence a week for five years. We've got by without it. What if we don' touch it - save it up. Can you work out how long that'd take to make ten pounds. You could do it you know. Now wouldn't that show'em?"

That night, drawing on his limited memory of mathematics learned thirty-five years earlier, he calculates that it should take him about a year to amass thirty-nine shillings. That means if he saves for a little over five years, he could do it. He could actually do it! He'll ask Sam Tricker where he might save his money so it earns a little interest. But he won't say why.

It makes a difficult decision a little less difficult; that is all. For some time, he'll occasionally find himself taking the long way home past what used to be Susan Subtle's house. And he feels sad.

Sam Tricker is concerned about two things and neither is about business. Now that is unusual! It is also a bit of a bother. Business problems can usually be solved one way or another. It is people who tend to pose the greatest problems of all. This time it involves two of the class of '63.

Henry Robinson farms in Combs. It is still his grand-father's farm, but he is a poor old thing these days and Henry, still ironically referred to as Tich, is in charge of the day-to-day management of the farm. To reach it from town, you have to cross the narrow bridge by Boulter's Mill. At least there is a bridge now. There are still people alive who can remember how sixty years before, a mail coach had lost its team of four horses crossing Combs water in a torrent. But it is a very narrow bridge - only one vehicle can pass at a time, and getting over into Combs can involve a wait. This time, it is worse than usual; far worse.

People literally throng the Market Place. Flags are flying, bells ringing. On enquiry it appears that 'brave Nelson' has done it again. Another victory over the French. All very well, but a bit irritating when you want to get somewhere. Men and women and children are swathed in flags of all nations and designs. As long as they aren't French flags, it doesn't seem to matter. A man is singing a new verse he has written to the tune of 'Rule Brittania', all about Nelson. It is all a little excessive. The Trickers seem to be the only ones leaving town in defiance of hundreds travelling the other way. It isn't easy making progress against the flow of traffic. Nobody seems prepared to give way - not today. Finally, they are across.

Then it is up the hill and around the corner and on until you begin to wonder whether you could still be in Combs. Sam and Mary have made this trip enough times to take it in their more than adequate stride.

This time, they find Henry the same 'hale-fellow-well-met' as ever and spend a comfortable and pleasant lunchtime together.

It is the following visit, just into the new year, when things prove rather less convivial. On this occasion, they are met by one of the maids who tells them 'Tich' is unwell and can't see them. Having travelled all that way, Sam Tricker is not so easily put off. But, on further investigation, it appears that Henry is rather worse than just 'unwell.'

"Smallpox?" Sam says disbelievingly. As he listens to the symptoms being itemised by the maid, it becomes just a list of words. Vile, unpleasant, terrifying, but just words. Malaise, nausea, muscle-cramps, pustules...

"Well are you sayin' we can't see him?"

"Apart from it in't safe, he say he don' want you to see 'im like this."

"Has a surgeon been sent for?"

"Yes sir, but when he see what it is, he don't want to stay long. He did leave a potion."

"I'll bet he did. And a hefty bill for the privilege."

But in spite of all their demands, Henry will not entertain them. Promising to find a surgeon who has either had the disease or been inoculated against it, they leave. They will not be the only ones refused entry over the next three difficult weeks. Neither friends nor family will be granted access.

Even the great love of his life, Debbie comes. But she too finds her way to Henry locked and barred.

So it is that the second of the class of '63 dies. And when they clear the room in which he has died, his few personal belongings are taken and given to his distraught parents.

There is a slight delay before the burial is allowed. Even finding someone for the laying-out poses problems. There is a certain disquiet. No-one wants to touch a body that is so clearly blighted and corrupt.

Oddly it turns out to be the only case of Smallpox in the area that winter. No-one knows how he had contracted it. In early February, the coffin will taken to the church at Combs, full two miles from the farm.

"We must stop doing this," says Isaac Pawsey to George Buckle. What he means is they only ever seem to meet at funerals.

"You might like to take charge of this," says old Henry Robinson. And he hands Isaac Pawsey a small book. It is the Bible they had each inscribed on leaving the charity school all those years ago. Inside, as a kind of page-marker he finds a piece of paper. It is a ten pound note. A second debt will be repaid.

If Henry hadn't died the way he did, Sam Tricker might have done more to find what had happened to Jerry Sharman. One morning, he had not appeared for work. Concerned about his health, colleagues had tried his room, only to discover it was empty. Jerry Sharman had gone. There had been never a hint that this might happen. Now Sam Tricker is irritated to say the least. He had helped him as best he could and now Jerry has just disappeared with not a word uttered.

As it is, the briefest of investigations leads Sam to pay a visit to the Brotherhood of Friends one Sunday morning. It is an odd experience - not like any church he has ever attended. He and Mary follow the ministry of Wesley. Gatherings at their church can be loud and inspiring. These people are altogether more calm and reflective. It feels foreign and perplexing. It is hard to tell when the service is over, but as people begin to leave, he takes the opportunity to ask if anyone has seen his old classmate. It is the same story. No story at all. No Jerry Sharman.

Chapter 23 ~ January 1801

At the turn of the year, it is customary in Suffolk to have a mild show of celebration. That is as far as it goes. It is not in our nature to be over-excessive or over-exuberant regarding such matters. To mark the end of a century or the beginning of another however, slightly more of an effort might be expected. But what is there to celebrate? England stands alone at war with France and is anticipating an invasion. A maritime alliance involving Russia, Prussia, Sweden and Denmark threatens our navy. True, an uneasy peace has been established in India: and nearer home... well, it is anyone's guess how long rebellion in Ireland will remain suppressed.

For most families - those without sons in the military - more basic issues are their prime concern. Finding food and fuel in the midst of the worst winter in living memory is all they can attend to now. Poverty has knocked harder than ever before. Parish overseers cannot cope. The Union workhouses are full to bursting and soup kitchens are springing up in the market towns of Suffolk. Great copper and pewter tureens, filled with whatever comes to hand, are boiled then simmered for hours before being made available to the starving. There is no shortage of takers.

But already questions are being asked about the effect feeding a concoction cooked in this manner might be having on already weakened paupers. The papers are full of it. Even the poor are aware of the hazards posed by cooking in copper and lead; but you have to eat something. Faced by the choice between starvation and poisoning by well-intentioned charitable providers, it is hardly surprising that for large numbers, 1800 and 1801 pass by with barely a thought being given to celebrating what are, after all, just dates.

For the remaining six of the class of '63, this like many other winters won't be easy, but they all know others who will suffer far worse. Over at Debenham, Martha Warren has been helping to collect food and unwanted clothing to distribute to the parish needy. Even the coats of the dying will be given a new home. Nothing must go to waste.

It has been a while since any of the Stonham 'boys' has been to visit. Their old schoolmaster has been anxious to catch up on their news. The weather has been to blame. Only when a brief warmer spell breaks through the interminable freeze does George Buckle finally find time to call.

Around the middle of the day when Thomas Warren has a break from his teaching duties, George bundles in, full of bluster and good stories as ever. This time however, he has even more of a tale to tell than usual, if anyone could believe the half of it.

Martha brings in tea on a tray, then leaves the men to chat.

"She still look proper bonny," George notes.

"What you mean is I look far too old to have a sprightly young thing like that to care for me. The funny thing is, she still gets embarassed about it. Would you believe but she's the only lady I know who claims publicly to be older than she actually is. She's told so many people she's five years older than what I know to be the case, that most of our friends and half her family now believe it. I think she does it to make me feel younger."

"Do it work?"

"Heavens, no! All that energy - it quite exhausts me just seeing how much she can find to fill her life with."

Now his eyes have adjusted to being in the dark room, George can see that the old schoolmaster is really showing his age. It is no great surprise when he thinks about it. He is still working, albeit part-time, and he not far short of his three-score years and ten. The master chunters to himself as he sips his tea and prepares to listen to all that George has to impart.

Truth to tell, George has been itching to come and tell this story. It has had to wait a while. And it will have to wait a few minutes longer. There must be a certain amount of news first - The master wants to know what are all the others doing, and so on. Like the prelude to the main event. And there is news to tell, as there always is after such an interval. The Trickers' latest venture, James Nunn's newest idea, Isaac Pawsey's increased acreage and suchlike. Thomas Warren needs a bit of help... he has forgotten who is married to whom and which children belong to which couple. He finds accurately remembering such matters difficult, and has to be reminded before he can be updated on much of it.

"You've still not heard from Jerry?" he asks.

"Naa," George answers. "Sam's right narked about it arter all he done for him, but he'll be back when he's ready."

He pauses, then adds, "It's odd but I'm not sure I didn't see him in Hadleigh last month. But it was a way off and prob'ly jus' someone like him. I called out to him, but he can't have heard or more likely it was someone else altogether. I did try to tell Sam, but he just say I'm a duzzy fule and what would Jerry be doin' in Hadleigh; so I shut up and didn' try to tell him no more."

"Hadleigh! Whatever were you doing there?"

"Well, thass what I come to tell you and a right good tale it is too, though my missus reckon I'm lucky to be alive."

"Go on then."

This is now the cue for George to tell of his experiences from a month before. And Mary Buckle is right: it could all have gone so horribly wrong.

"As you know, old Mr. Studd died and his son now run the Magpye. My new master, young Mr. Studd, he say to me one day, 'How'd you like to go to London?'"

"'Not much,' I told him, seeing as last time I got out of the place about as quick as I could, but then he say he have a cousin who run a cart, regular-like from Hadleigh to London. All his drivers are off sick and he need a good man with horses to help him take a cartload of stuff to Stepney."

"I hear the London road can be quite dangerous."

"Indeed it can. The Stowmarket coach was robbed just the other week. We knew we had to take precautions like - so, Mr. De'ath - thass Mr. Studd's cousin's name. He spells it 'Death', but calls it 'Dee-Ath'. Well, he arranged to travel in company with Mr. Garrad's Colchester waggon. Footpads and highwaymen and the like don't usually attack when there's more than one. Thass what he say. But I know now thass a load of ol' squit."

"Did something go wrong on the way?"

"Funny enough, the journey there was right as rain. We got there easy. Took all day of course: dark when we started, dark when we finished. Had to change horses twice. Not so often as the Mail Coaches, but often enough. It's funny, I complain about the Pye Inn, but I'll tell you, it's a palace compared to some of the places I saw along the road to London. I'd feel ashamed to work in some of them.

We had just two horses to pull the cart; Mr. Garrad needed four for his waggon. Right loaded it was. As soon as we got to Stepney, we unloaded; got paid. Spent the night in a rough ol' place. Had to share a room with Garrad's waggoner. Coo, he dun't half snore! Worse'n the missus. Anyway, we started back the next morning. Thass when you know to look out. Cos *they* notice carts what go out full an' come back empty - *they* guess there's money aboard. Comin' back, we tried to pack the cart with empty boxes and to cover them up, but that wun't no good - the cart was much lighter so the horses pulled easier and *they* notice things like that."

"Were you armed?"

"Not me," George laughed, "I'd be no good with a pistol or a shotgun - most prob'ly shoot meself. But Mr. De'ath, he had a horse-pistol loaded with slugs. An' it's just as well he did!"

"Were you attacked?"

"'Tween Brentwood an' Shenfield, Mr. Garrad got a bit of a way ahead of us. We was meant to stay together but his horses runned ahead of ours. Then it happened. I couldn't see much at first, but it looked like a tall man in a white shirt or frock darted from behind a hedge and thrust his pistol at the waggoner's head. Then the blighter struck it down, but luckily it just flashed in the pan and didn't go off. It didn't stop him demanding money though, and before you knew it the two on'em began fighting. Mr. Garrad wun't a lot of good, just climbed down and got out the way.

"What did you do?"

"I had to mind the horses, but Mr. De'ath, as we got closer, he primed his pistol and waited for the two to part so he could fire and get a shot at the man. He was fearful, you see of shooting Mr. Garrad's man. Then the waggoner whacked him one and as soon as the two were apart for a moment, Mr. De'ath fired. He reckon he hit the robber, though I didn't see no blood and I have my doubts. He moved fast enough when he runned off over the heath."

"You had no trouble after that?"

"I should hope not. I were shaking so much I could scarce hold the reins. We stuck together arter that, I can tell you. It was whully scary at the time, but it wun't a bad story, eh?"

"George, it is a wonderful story. You should write it down."

"I don't need to - it were all in the Journal last week. They didn't mention me of course, just the owners of the vehicles. My missus say I in't never to go to London agin. There's some rum owd folks there, I can tell you."

The story George tells his old schoolmaster is fresh enough to be fairly faithful to events, though he still finds it impossible to describe the true horror he experienced at the time. He doesn't like to admit to being reluctant to take to the road alone any more, or the fact he sometimes wakes in the middle of the night shaking.

But it is too good a mardle to leave there, and many an evening in the Magpye Inn, he'll be bought drinks on the strength of its re-telling. That, of course, is when the embellishment begins. One by one, the class of '63 will each hear a slightly different version. All except for Jerry Sharman, of course. He is still missing.

Chapter 24 ~ Spring 1804

He turns up again - of course he does, like a fractured farthing. What is more, he does not seem in the slightest bit concerned that he might have inconvenienced a few friends along the way. Jerry Sharman is back. And he brings with him the same air of mystery about him that has always appeared to be part of his demeanour. Truth to tell, there hasn't been a lot of mystery; not really. Instead, a rash decision and he has disappeared for five years. That is about all there is to say on the matter.

Banking. Well, in a way. And in a way it makes sense. He may only have had two years with Mr. Warren, but he was always quick on the uptake and had learned fast. Added to which, four years working for the Trickers and he can add up a sheet of figures rather better than the next man. Then there is the business of bankers. The Quakers - who own most of the banks in Suffolk at this time? That's right, the Quakers. The fact nobody had spotted was that he had the opportunity, through their assorted meetings, of coming into contact with a lot of rich and influential people. All you have to add to that cauldron of possibilities has to be the newly-acquired confidence that had come from his work in Stowmarket. He could sell himself and his abilities

So, why is he back now? Enough of it, you might suppose. Sam Tricker has words to say on the matter...

"They might say Jerry Sharman can't stick at narthin'."

"They might say Jerry Sharman likes to get out and about and experience life and all it has to offer instead of stickin' around malty old Stowmarket for the rest of his life."

"So what'll you do now you are back?"

"Jerry grins. You'll enjoy this. I'm tally-man for the Navigation, except I can count more than the number of fingers on my two hands, so I don't need a tally-stick. I can keep records of what travels as far as Ipswich - sacks of malt and the like - sometimes travel with it and see the right number of bags get safely aboard a ship in Ipswich dock. I have a horse in waiting that my opposite number in Ipswich will take back when he comes here. That horse! It's done that trip so many times, you can sit astride it and let it take you the whole way without a word. Now that is what I call a job."

"Better'n what I had to offer once?" says Sam. I s'pose it's another case where your Brotherhood in't a bad bunch to know?"

"It helps. They know I'm prob'ly honest. Can't have a tallyman that can't be trusted."

Sam Tricker knows that to his own misfortune. There has to be some advantage of one man taking charge of the whole shipment until it lies safely in the hold of the receiving ship.

"Sam, I'll allers be grateful, you know that. That was then; this is now. Tomorrow, who knows?"

"Who knows, indeed. You know Jerry, I think you enjoy this."

"What, bein' a tallyman?" Jerry is now laughing at him. Few dare do that these days.

"No, bein' a man of mystery. Someone who can disappear and then just pop up again like a jack-in-the-box. You like surprisin' folks."

Perhaps he has been strutting a bit - like the fighting cocks remembered from their youth.

"Yer know when I was small, my mum took me to the fair at Mendlesham on Whit Monday. There was a man - a magician in a tent all by itself at the edge of the field. He was a real mystery man, I can tell you. He only done one show that afternoon. Real magic, he said. Making things disappear and reappear and so on. I went on at my mother, so she paid for us to go in, and it was worth every penny. He was the best any onnus had ever seen. Then right at the end, he stepped inside a hoop that he raised above his head. It had candy-stripe linen cloth attached. And he kept raising it until we couldn't see his hands no more. Then he let it drop. And you know what, he weren't there no more. Now that was magic!"

"Gaa, a trick," says Sam.

"Course it was, but for the life of me, I don't know how he did it. Still don't. But I loved that man of mystery. I used to dream of him at nights. I wanted to be him. I wanted the feeling of power it must give you to be that man of mystery. Father said I shouldn't wish for what in't real and in't natural. 'Live with what the Lord give you,' he'd-a-said."

"Halleluyah!" says Sam, and Jerry echoes him, before closing with, "But I'd still like to know how he done it."

* * * * *

James Nunn has had an accident. He, being of a practical nature, would not agree, but puts it down to carelessness on his part. He has been kicked on the head by a horse. In way, it was bound to happen, spending a lifetime with horses. It is an occupational hazard that threatens the best of them. Even George Buckle who claims, most of the time, to be at one with the horse has been a victim more than once. Because 'most of the time' isn't good enough. One unguarded moment is all it takes. It is all it has taken to place James Nunn into that precarious position somewhere between life and death.

Carried home by cart and drifting in and out of consciousness he has, for some time, been the charge of his long-suffering wife. This is not the first time he has fallen foul of an accident at work. Hot metal is unpredictable stuff. So, unfortunately, are hot-tempered animals.

However careful you might be, sooner or later something

like this is sure to happen. You shoe horses, hammer harness, manufacture fittings for carriages and carts, forge chains and mechanisms that will be attached to horses before completion is confirmed... An accident waiting for its inevitable moment.

But he is made of such stuff that will ensure a slow recovery. Now the swelling has gone down and much of the bruising eased, he has become fit enough to be visited by a host of well-wishers including friends from the past. The parson comforts him by making it clear that God intends him to spend more time on this earth, so perhaps he should put it to good use. That sets him thinking.

A curved blue-black scar will remain as a reminder and a warning to take more by way of care and less by way of assumption. Oddly, it sits beside an older paler scar, but that belongs to a time so long ago, it has almost been forgotten. He will also be plagued by headaches from time to time, an affliction that will never entirely leave him.

Mary Nunn has run the full gamut of emotions this time. At first distraut, despairing of any real hope of his recovery, then to fussing over him more mother hen-like than she ever has with their children. Finally, she is starting to question whether he needs to assume the role of invalid any longer: her patience was never her strongest point.

Mary says he is getting under her feet, though nothing could be further from the truth. He has barely moved from his chair for weeks. His mind, however, has been more active than it has been in a long while. Now, having time to reflect, he has been casting glances at his collection. Mary Nunn calls it 'that heap of old scrap' that lies beside the shed in what she struggles to maintain as a garden. It's not her fault. There are two small children to care for and now a husband she disdainfully describes as being, "not much better than a cripple." He must be better, if she can talk to him in that way once more.

His collection. Metal has been the defining item of his life. There are many kinds here. What might appear to the layman to be a heap of old scrap has been carefully sorted into copper and tin, brass and iron. There are also fragments of tempered steel. More precious metals are there too in smaller quantities. All have been lovingly kept for the day when time will permit them to be reworked in ways that may be far removed from their original purpose.

It is hard when you are working all the hours God sends to make time for such matters. Now, for once in his life, he has had the time to reflect and again be truly creative.

There are moments when the headaches strike when he can bear no such thought, nor any thought at all. Then, all he can do is lie back in a darkened room and wait for the pain to ease. But slowly these bouts are becoming fewer. In between times, he has been sketching ideas. Then, he knows, when he feels able, he will make the short journey to Mendlesham where he knows a white-smith from whom he has further skills to learn. How might he join different metals? What heat, what substances, what time?

This is when he casts his mind back full forty years to those days in school when, as boys, they were encouraged to let their imagination flourish. Perhaps now he can see his way clear to building a seed drill the like of which they had planned all those years before. Call it part of his recovery perhaps. That is how how he sells the idea to his wife. It isn't a new idea of course, but as with his earlier successes, he can refine it and make it his own.

Then, when old friends do visit, they generally find him surrounded by 'bits of old scrap' and a few sketched ideas on torn pieces of paper. But as he is keen to point out, one man's heap of scrap is another man's pot of gold. Though it takes the imagination of a James Nunn to recognise that.

The seed drill is slowly being born. It is hard to know how many of the class of '63, if any, really remember the origin of this idea some forty years before, but true to form, George Buckle's comment is, "'T'wunt work. My ol' man could cast seed better'n that ol' thing." Apart from the fact his ol' man has been dead for a number of years, it is unlikely he could ever have sown a field with such efficiency of purpose as James Nunn's creation. Again, whilst it will never make him rich, it will further enhance his reputation and ensure his family should live in greater comfort than the Nunns in previous generations. But that is a whole other story.

Chapter 25 ~ August 1804

Malt. There had been maltings in Stowmarket for years. That was before. Since the navigation has arrived, and you can transport goods quickly and cheaply to Ipswich, they have propagated. Now not only the long-established families like Rout and Rust own maltings, but a whole lot of newer ones, many with no tradition in the craft.

In reality, malting is quite simple. You take a quantity of grain, usually barley, and persuade it with a little moisture and heat to begin germinating. Rub off the green shoots and you have malt all ready for drying. By 1804, the drying floors and malting towers are visible all over town. The Trickers can number five within a hundred yards of their home. Then as it dries, comes the malty aroma: there are worse smells, but it hangs across the town especially on still days. On windy days, the breeze carries the scent up to the closest villages; Stowupland, Old Newton and Haughley. No wonder the likes of country boys like James Nunn and Isaac Pawsey find coming to Stowmarket overpowering.

But with new maltings companies opening yearly, the drift from the land is beginning. Tom Brett has worked on farms for almost the whole of his life. Now, he is shuffling and bagging malt and carting it to the Navigation Wharf to be winched aboard barges bound for Ipswich. The smell is there all the time now. It is on his skin, in his clothes, even impregnating his hair through his cap. It doesn't matter how much you bathe, you reek of malt. Not an unpleasant smell, but it is there. And if he ventures far enough out of Stowmarket to escape the malty air that hangs over the town, he still can't lose it. All he can smell these days is malt. All his food tastes of it. But the money is better; the work is there, on his doorstep; you don't get laid off when the weather is bad. In spite of all these considerations, there is an inner sadness when he remembers summers bringing home the harvests past.

Gambling. If it isn't one thing, then it's another. As if Rachel Brett hadn't had enough in her life to cope with! That man - he'd bet on anything! There are plenty around, of course, prepared to accept his money. She has tried her best to make sure he has few pence in his pockets but he can spirit money up from somewhere if he thinks there is the chance of a good thing. Don't blame the schoolmaster! Hadn't he gone out of his way all those years ago to demonstrate that gamblers are fools who just can't wait to be parted from their money? No, Thomas Brett has to be held entirely responsible for his own irresponsible behaviour.

"You owe the man how much?" she shrieks, hardly able to contain herself.

He is standing there, waving a slip of paper like Jack trying to explain to his mother that he has sold their cow for handful of beans. In a way, it was all so horribly predictable. There are four drinking houses in Stowupland Street. The Pickerel isn't the cheapest, but there is an upstairs room where the publican John Marriott allows the likes of Tom Brett and others to play Faro or games of Hazard for small amounts of money. The Pickerel sits on the Stowupland side of the river. Amongst those hostelries on the other side, the Barge is definitely the cheapest but, as locals could tell you, there for your twopence you can get a pint, a pie and a thick ear. Most of the Stowmarket natives give it a wide berth.

On the night in question late in the month of August, three other men were playing. They included Webster Adams, which might have seemed odd. He owned a beer-house further up the street. But his wife kept a tight eye on him there, so he drank a number of nights at the Pickerel. That was when all the trouble arose.

"Ten pounds - Oh Thomas!"

He knows he is in trouble when she calls him Thomas. He tries again to retrieve the situation. That is where the piece of paper comes in.

"...Well, it was only eight pounds but Mr. Adams said he'd sell me this ticket for two pounds and I could win it all back again. It's a ticket for the National Lottery. They're tryin' to raise money for the war with France."

"I know what it is. It's one of those stupid things that nobody but rich buggers buy and nobody ever wins."

"I might win - I could win twenty thousan' pounds."

"No you couldn't."

"It say so on the ticket. I could."

"No you couldn't. I know I can't read like you can, but I know what you got there. Now you read it." Then, to her astonishment, he puts the ticket first at a normal reading distance, then ever closer to his eyes, before dangling it as far away as his reach will allow.

"It's too small print, I can't quite get the gist of it."

"Are you telling me your sight is goin'?"

"Not exactly. I'm fine when I'm outdoors, lookin' 'cross fields, but..."

"...But you don't do that no more." Rachel is beginning to understand what must have been going on in that befuddled brain.

"I could get spectacles for reading."

"You coulda done before you spent more money than we ever got in our lives. Jus' where d'yer think you are goin' to find ten pounds to pay Mr. Adams?"

"I thought perhaps that money in the bank to pay for the Bible from school..."

"Oh, Thomas, jus' think. Thass taken you how long to save that money? Eight years? Ten years? An' you lost it in jus' one night."

Then she stops as a thought crosses her mind.

"If you can't see proper close-up, how did you see them cards?"

"'Tin't easy. But I can tell which are pictures and which are spots, and pictures is usually better than spots. Spots go all blurry, 'specially the red ones. I hoped I wouldn't get a hand with lots of red dots."

"So in actual fact, you have been playing cards almost blind. Oh that's right clever that is! You coulda had a hand full of aces and not have known. You Lummock! You woolly-hidded dorble!"

"Here, go steady," says Tom trying to rescue a little pride from the situation. "I am your husband."

"You're sorft in the hid, thass what you are, Tom Brett. An' as for Mr. Webster Adams, takin' advantage like that. You wait till I see his missus!"

"But he done me a favour with the lottery ticket."

"Only because he'd bought it and was afraid his wife would find out. Anyway, it is not a lottery ticket." Seeing the blank look on his face, she continues, "It is the sixteenth share in a lottery ticket. Thass all. I've seen 'em before. An' as for winning, well, you can forget that."

If ever a man looked depressed, it is this one right at this moment. Rachel is not yet ready to be even vaguely sympathetic. "Hev you give any thought as to how you get that money out of the bank?"

No he hasn't. That has been all Sam Tricker's doing. His bank... Alexanders in Needham... solid, secure, safe; run by a Quaker family. Bevan's bank in Stowmarket, he had said, would wind up in trouble. Sam knows about these things. Therefore, as a favour, he opened an account in Tom's name and every few weeks has made a deposit. It's surely worth at least ten pounds by now.

But, how is he supposed to get it out?

"You'll hev to ask Sam to do it for you." says Rachel.

"But he'll want to know what I need it for," says Tom.

"He never knew what it was bein' saved for. You never told him."

"He muss know: ten pounds, thass what we all had to find."

"So, you tell 'im you bin a bit of a prat. What can he do?"

"He can give me that look."

Tom Brett knows only too well how everyone coming into contact with Sam Tricker dreads the withering look he has cultivated in later years. He never stamps his feet nor raises his voice, but he can reduce a fifty year-old man to a quivering jelly with that look. It conveys hurt, disappointment, contempt, disdain and finally a sense of disgrace and humiliation. Even Rachel has to understand he would do almost anything to avoid that.

"Give me a few days, an' I'll see if anything else comes to mind," Rachel says, more in hope than expectation.

"I 'spec he'll wait a few days for his money."

"Well if he dun't, send him to talk to me. Mr. Webster Adams indeed!"

In reality nothing is done; nothing actually happens. Tom half expects the next step will be in Rachel's hands. But she seems prepared to wait a while. Perhaps she is trying to force the issue with the man responsible. She is no longer sure this is really her husband's fault. One benefit of all this is the talking. For days, and for the first time in years, they talk - they talk about how they feel about everything; not just the gambling debt.

"I really miss not having the kids around no more. Oh I know they come and visit and have their own lives to live, but even this little place seems too big. I miss not knowing about my other boy over in Colchester. For all I know he could be joining up as a soldier and goin' off to fight Boney. We've heard nothin' and it don't feel right."

All this comes tumbling out one evening, and a whole lot more besides.

"You're not happy at work, are you?" Rachel says, not so much asking him as telling him she knows where his heart is and it is now time to make a change."

"To tell the truth, I hate most of it - cooped up in those malty ol' buildings with their malty ol' smell. The only good time is takin' the cart to the dock to load up the barges, an' I feel like jus' jumpin' aboard and stayin' out in the open air all the way to Ipswich. But then I'd only have to come back."

"So change. You've worked on farms most of your life - go back to working on farms."

"The money 'in't so good."

"There's only us now. We don't need a lot of money."

"There's times when it's really hard."

"An' times when it's heavenly. You want to go back - go back to Stonham. Talk to Isaac. Thass what friends are for."

"I s'pose I might. Yeah, thass a right good idea."

Just then, (or anytime before or after) - a man knows he has a debt, he knows it has to be paid, but the longer time passes since anyone last spoke of it... and he can begin to believe that there really is a God up there on his side... That the debt might actually disappear, or that he imagined it all in the first place. That maybe Mr. Webster Adams will never come back demanding his ten pounds, and he, Thomas Brett, will not have to suffer the formidable stare of Samuel Tricker.

As if... That hope lasts all of twelve days. Then, there is a knock at the door, followed by the corporeal frame of Mr. Adams. Dressed for a rather grander surrounding, he sports a new green and yellow-braided coat with a high collar. He doesn't sit down and he isn't invited to. He seems to be considering what to say. When he does speak, his tone is remarkably conciliatory.

"That debt - I think I may have been a little unfair to you. Eight pounds the poorer, and I foisted a ticket on you to make matters worse - It was never my intention, you understand, but I chose a bad moment."

Rachel has heard a noise from where she is upstairs and descends to see what this is all about.

"Anyway, I thought as I was a wee bit aggressive that night, I could make you a more-than-fair offer. Sell the ticket back to me at... say, five pounds, and your debt to me will be halved. Now do we have a deal?"

Slightly suspicious of the newly magnanimous Mr. Adams, Tom isn't quite sure how to respond. Rachel, behind the door, has no such doubts.

"If you feel that bad Mr. Adams, how about cancelling the debt entirely?"

"But he only paid me two pounds for it," stammers the city gent in front of them.

"You played cards with a man who couldn't even see well enough to know what cards were in his hand, so it wouldn't be too much, surely to appeal to your better nature."

Webster Adams' better nature is a creature that has stayed well-hidden for many years, so it is to their even greater surprise when he finally seems to realise when he is beaten and says, "Yes, of course, debt cancelled. Come man, give me the ticket and we'll shake on it."

"I don't think so." That is Rachel. "I think we'll keep the ticket and we'll pay you the ten pounds just as soon as we can." Then just to prove she means her word, she waves the ticket at him and tucks it into the snuggest part of her blouse she can find.

He might possibly have played that game more wisely, but in all likelihood, Rachel would still have rumbled him. Clearly, he's not a very good actor. Had he not been playing with a half-blind man that night, it would have been only too clear that he's not a very good card-player either.

"Too keen by half. Couldn't hide the gleam in his eyes," says Rachel. It's a fact. Even if his face hadn't given him away, the slump in his ample form would. She hadn't even needed a gambler's instinct to spot a fraud like that. Still, Tom tells her he wouldn't want to play cards against her. He wouldn't have a chance.

It is therefore no great surprise to discover, the unlikely, if not impossible has happened. They are the proud owners of a sixteenth share of one thousand pounds. Though Mr. Adams swears blind he had no knowledge of this when making his offer, Tom says it was all too clear that he was just pissing into the wind and sooner or later was about to get a bit of his own back. Rachel agrees, though in less colourful terms. What this large piece of luck - the largest in their lives - means is, Tom will get his spectacles, some clothes that no longer smell of malt and Rachel her first new dress in years.

In Conclusion ~ June 1807

In a tiny cottage, away across the fields, Rachel Brett is tidying up before receiving a visitor or two. She finds the small case which holds the precious spectacles that has required two visits by her husband Tom to Mr. Lyons in Carr Street in Ipswich before they could be made ready for their new owner. The second of these journeys had been arranged by Jerry Sharman who had taken him by the Gipping Navigation through a series of locks. Tom had spent the night away from home; about the only time in his married life he has - apart from the occasional night on an alehouse floor. He was mighty relieved to get back the following day, bearing the watchmaker & optician's remarkable creation. Rachel can hardly believe that such things exist. She has to keep taking them out and examining them. Today there will be Mary Pawsey, Mary Buckle and Mary Nunn to entertain. She will show them, and they too will marvel. Heavens, friends to afternoon tea! It is almost genteel!

Truth to tell, it is the wives now who are more able to keep the friendship going. There are always too many reasons why the others can't find the time.

Jerry Sharman has just returned from visiting Mr Warren in Debenham and the news is grave. One by one, he tells the others and, one by one, they will make their way one last time to see the old man.

How old is he? Nobody is very sure. George says that the next time he goes, he'll ask. For George has always believed he was the most special of all the master's pupils. He tells him.

"I was the best boy you ever taught," he announces on that last visit.

"Describe what you mean by 'best', George."

"Well, the best at reading, writing, mathematics ...oh, and making maps of course."

"I'm sorry to disappoint you George, but you probably weren't the best at reading, almost certainly weren't the best at writing and quite definitely weren't the best at mathematics..." At this, Thomas Warren experiences a spasm of coughing and it is a while before he is able to add, "...but it is very possible you might have been the best at the making of maps." That is enough for George and he can return to his home in Little Stonham contented. His younger brother William may be fighting for liberty half a world away, but at least George can lay claim to a tiny piece of immortality right here in Suffolk.

* * * * *

Now, just weeks later, they come to bury the Master, his own wife having died two years earlier, a shock for which he was ill-prepared. The children from his earlier marriage will not be here, but countless others of his children will. Perhaps most special of all are the survivors from that class long ago, George, James, Isaac, Jerry, Thomas and Samuel.

Unable to work without Martha at his side, he left the school in 1805. The idea had always been for them to retire into a house in the village. They had watched for the right place together, and when it came for sale, they had found the money, in the belief it would benefit both of them.

For two years, he has merely mourned within its walls.

That self-same property will now be willed to his wife's nephew, John Palmer, the nearest to a son he has known. So his own children are not completely forgotten, there will be ten pounds for each. It seems a little derisory, but in recent years, he would probably not have known them had he passed them in Gracechurch Street.

A few old friends come from Stonham: George Bird, who was taught to swim by the Master one summer in the lake at Deerbolts Hall: Edmund Tydeman, one of a number of brothers all of whom attended the school before going on to farm in Earl Stonham: But many of those he knew then are now already in the ground. Far more attend from Debenham.

George half-hoped he might say a word or two at the funeral, but the class of '63 are not known here, and why should they consider themselves special? He, like the others follows the procession to the interment at a respectful distance. Beside the open grave, a stone already stands to mark the last resting place of Martha Warren. George is not the only one of the group to note that the gravestone records her age at death to have been 61, making her four years older than she really was. He grins to himself as he works the numbers in his head.

At the sending-off that follows, it is left to Sam Tricker to remind the others, a time has been called.

Later that year, James Nunn and George Buckle, representing all of them, will hand over the remaining sixty pounds to Samuel Bird in settlement of a promise that can no longer be ignored. The words each of them was encouraged to write in the front of a Bible have not been forgotten. Not by the dead and not by the living. Though now diminished by two, the class of '63 will be united as no other group attending school at Earl Stonham ever will again.

*　　*　　*　　*　　*

It is the faintest rustle in the ditch that tells him someone is there. His eyes might have let him down, but his ears are still good enough. Tom Brett is on his way to do a little hoeing for his master Isaac Pawsey. Both sides of the wide ditch are lined by stands of pollarded and coppiced trees. Down in the ditch, he finds Benjamin, Isaac Pawsey's young nephew.

"Now what might you be doin', master Benjamin?"

"Oh, Mr. Brett, I'm breakin' off a stick."

"Not that 'un you wun't," Tom Brett says.

"I'm very strong. I go to school now you know."

"Ooh, I'm not sayin' you in't strong. I'm jus' sayin' thass the wrong sorta stick. It's hazel, you see; don't break, jus' bends."

Then, taking a knife from his pocket and opening it, he searches around the new growth at the base of the coppice. Then, he puts a small nick low down on another stick.

"Now let's see if we can break this one." The two of them pull the cane downwards until with a snap, it comes free.

"Thass ash, that 'un. Ash snaps, hazel don't. Simple as that." The boy is most impressed and watches Tom prune surplus leaves and twigs from the top of the stick, leaving just a notch for the boy's thumb.

"How did you know that, Mr. Brett?" asks the boy.

Tom Brett smiles as he thinks about years past.

"Some'un musta taught me, a long time ago." he says.

George Buckle, on retirement is believed to have moved to Creeting St. Mary where he died in 1818.
A number of Thomas Bretts are recorded locally. Our Tom Brett is probably the one who was buried at Stowmarket in 1817.
Both Samuel and Mary Tricker were buried in Stowmarket on the same day in June 1834.
Isaac Pawsey was buried at Earl Stonham in 1837. He was living at Mendlesham at the time of his death.
James Nunn, it is believed, moved to Drinkstone, where he ended his days as a non-conformist and may have been buried at Rattlesden Baptist church.
The final resting place of Jacob, known as Jerry, Sharman remains a mystery.

The Class of '63

Notes

Much of this book was written by history. Where possible, I have stuck to what evidence remains of the characters and events in this story. Where that has not been possible, I have followed such details as I know and come up with what I regard as the most plausible sequence of events. Virtually every person mentioned in this book actually existed at the time described. A few events have been moved a few miles to colour the story. In other words, this is a true story... apart from the bits I had to invent.

Significant documents to be found at Ipswich Record Office:
FB23/M1/1 Earl Stonham Charity School records
FB23/E1/2 & 3 Earl Stonham Churchwarden's Accounts
FB23/G6/3, 4 & 5 Earl Stonham Overseers' Books
FB23/D1... Earl Stonham parish registers
ADA2/CB1/1 Bosmere & Claydon Union House register from 1765
FB232/A1/2 Hamlet Watling's album of Earl Stonham church

Introduction

Candler Bird is easily identified from 18th century documents as one of the great 'movers and shakers' of Earl Stonham - Overseer of the poor, Churchwarden, Charity Trustee, etc. The coffee-houses named are also well-documented. *'The Sacred & Profane History of Bury'* (pub. 1998) by Peter Bishop describes in particular the Widow's Coffee House which must have been close to where the Cathedral Shop is today. The school at Needham Market had been founded in 1632 with high aspirations, but fell short and offered a fairly basic education to poor free scholars as well as a few fee-payers. See *'History of Needham Market'* by E.W. Platten (1925).

Thomas Warren was born around 1732, but there are many of this name in Suffolk and I can't actually identify his place of birth. He is almost certainly not the Thomas Warren, map-maker of Bury, though he may have been related. He married Elizabeth Marsh at Earl Stonham in 1756. They were both named as 'of this parish' though he cannot have lived there very long before that.

PART 1
Chapter 1

Early maps show part of Middlewood Green was still common land. All gipsy names used in this chapter are taken from gipsy family names known to be travelling in East Anglia at the time.

Thomas Brett was the third child born to Thomas and Mary (Garnham). He had been baptised at Earl Stonham in June 1756. The 'race-course' beside the stream near the church is named as such on early maps, though it must have been quite a short track. The character 'Morgan' (a.k.a. 'Regan') is taken from an almost contemporary account in the Ipswich Journal (August 1764). He was wanted across several counties.

George Buckle was probably the son of George Buckle of Earl Stonham who appears to have married twice, first to Mary (Groome), then to Martha (?). I have not found George's baptism, though he must have been born around 1753, when his sister Ann was baptised. He and Henry Robinson were the eldest in the class, having been taught for a year before the others joined them.

Several Earl Stonham rectors were also rectors of Cambridge parishes and rarely attended. A succession of curates actually managed the parish. Rev. Syer was one of many. The wall-paintings were finally revealed again in the late 19th century, but unfortunately, most have not survived, though Hamlet Watling painted pictures of them before they disappeared.

What is now called Earl Stonham House was once the site of the rectory. Remains of a substantial moat indicate a fine residence stood there before the present Victorian dwelling.

Isaac Pawsey was the fourth child of Jacob and Mary (?). He was baptised at Earl Stonham in January 1756. Several local parishes (e.g. Brundish) have detailed regulations regarding the administration of gleaning.

Chapter 2

Deerbolts Hall was the seat of the Driver family, but their tenure here was coming to an end. We know that the Bird family moved into Deerbolts around this time as several members of the family were born there. There are vague references to the Sharman family being Quakers. A Quaker meeting house and graveyard was at Duncan's (now known as the Tan Office) at Mendlesham Green.

Jerry Sharman (occasionally 'Sherman') was probably baptised Jacob Sharman, the third child of Thomas & Elizabeth (Bishop) at Earl Stonham in March 1753.

I have chosen the name 'Mrs. Bugg' for the housekeeper as she was a widow living in Creeting All Saints at the time.

It is hard to imagine how Deerbolts Hall looked before its Victorian make-over, but I have attempted to draw from other similar grand houses of the time. The grounds are still very much as I have described them.

Candler Bird (born 1706) married Mary (Sheldrake), who was 22 years his junior, in 1748. They baptised ten children, three of them called Mary.

The robbery of the toll-booth at Stonham Parva actually happened in August 1764 (Ipswich Journal)

Chapter 3

John Coat(e)s appears to be the only one of the class not of labouring stock. He was baptised seventh child of John and Mary (?) at Earl Stonham in November 1755.

Medieval morality plays had fallen out of favour, but were beginning to be revived at this time. The lines quoted here are slight variations on the originals.

Martha Palmer was baptised at Earl Stonham in 1746, but appears to have been living in Stonham Aspal by 1763. I have not completed the family link with the Coats family.

Lands in Stowupland and Stowmarket raised revenue for Earl Stonham charities.

Henry Robinson was the eldest son of Henry and Mary (Brown) and was baptised in Earl Stonham in July 1753.

Samuel Tricker was the fourth child of William & Mary (?) and was baptised on Christmas Day 1755 at Earl Stonham.

James Nunn was the fifth child of Joshua & Mary (Baker) and was baptised at Earl Stonham in July 1755.

Chapter 4

The deaths from the Nunn family are taken from the burial register for Earl Stonham. How they died is unknown. Coroners' reports from the time supplied information regarding how many people died.

Articles quoted are taken from magazines and journals of the time. The Mendlesham School advertisement appeared in the Ipswich Journal in May 1764.

The trip to Ipswich refers to an entertainment advertised at the time. Coaches ran from the Pye Inn at Stonham Parva to Ipswich. The early Home

Medical book by John Theobald was advertised in local papers throughout 1764.

Chapter 5

The Margery Bedingfield murder case was very much the crime of the century and was bound to have been much discussed. Newspapers from 1763 onwards advertised broadsheets and broadsides on the subject. The Higgins family were carriers at Stonham Aspal over several generations.

William Bacon of Diss was finally arrested in July 1764, as reported in the Ipswich Journal.

Chapter 6

Jemmy Chambers, the wandering poet is recorded in a host of places. It was fashionable, even 'romantic' to recognise talent in the meanest of men. Chambers received sponsorship and support but wandered freely around Mid-Suffolk, bedding down in barns and penning his verses. He certainly came to Thorndon and Wetheringsett; maybe to Stonham. (Read more in 'Frolic, Fervour & Fornication' by Pip Wright). The lines quoted are authentic.

No pictures survive of the old Guildhall. A possible hint of what it might have been like exists in a few villages in Suffolk, though all have been much restored.

Old Southgate and others putting fresh gravel on the church paths appear as a regular payment in the Earl Stonham Churchwarden's accounts.

'Six and ninepence' is a character from an advert in the Ipswich Journal in October 1764. In that case, he had strayed from his people in Harwich. Mr. Williams was known to have resided at Waltham Hall a little later than this.

Chapter 7

There are plenty who will remember the area around the Guildhall Cottages as suffering from regular flooding. Early maps call it 'The Wallows'. Only quite recently has this improved.

It was normal for villages with charity schools to seek apprenticeships for their departing pupils. These could be at some distance from home. No apprenticeship indentures survive for Earl Stonham from this time. However, nearby Stowmarket has a host of them including links with London. As will be shown, George Buckle returns whilst his younger (half-?) brother William will end up in Canada as a soldier (British Regimental Registers of Service).

Chapter 8

The letter to the editor that is quoted was published in the Ipswich Journal in November 1764. Bells were regularly rung for Royal recoveries after all manner of sicknesses. Mr. Garnham was Earl Stonham sexton at this time.

Corn prices were the main concern that winter and the following summer. Dunnington and Cook were millers over generations in Earl Stonham and Stonham Aspal. The Earl Stonham mill was long past its best, but struggled on until 1824 when a new windmill was built near the old one. The two must have stood together for a while, as early maps describe 'Stonham Mills'.

The doctors named in these chapters - Cooper and Palgrave are taken from the Overseers' accounts. They were sometimes paid by the parish for attending to sick paupers. Diphtheria and Scarlatina were major killers of children for some time to come.

Chapter 9

Hiring sessions were advertised in the Ipswich Journal. The Pye (Magpie) Inn at Stonham Parva was the usual hiring place, both at Michaelmas and in early Summer for harvest hirings. It was common to demand attendance at the parish church as a condition of hiring.

Candler Bird's paperwork, referred to here, is remarkable. It is beautifully crafted, with elegant and artistic flare that goes way beyond what must have been expected.

The descriptions of swimming and skating at Livermere and Ampton are taken from slightly later articles in the Bury Post.

References to the new Trustees and sums accounted for are taken from Churchwarden's accounts for Earl Stonham. The Bibles given out on leaving the school may have been donated here. Other charity schools such as Holton in Suffolk certainly did this and insisted on the writing of such a promise.

Warning adverts about poaching at Stonham appeared around this time in the Ipswich Journal. I have no knowledge of any following prosecutions. Ipswich Races, with accompanying cock-fights, was a big attraction for those who could afford to go.

The crossroads suicide was one of a number of such cases reported around this time. Briefs read out in church were a way of spreading news and raising a few pence each week for good causes.

A few lists of collections can be seen in Suffolk Record Offices. None survive from Earl Stonham. The Wattisham story (Downing family) would have been familiar to all of the congregation at that time and probably prompted generous donations.

Chapter 10

William Scapy and Candler Bird were leading citizens of Earl Stonham at this time. The move away from parish poor-houses to union work-houses was underway and would have been their responsibility.

The Ipswich Journals for Summer 1765 were full of reports of the destruction and riots surrounding the building of workhouses at Nacton and Bulc(h)amp near Blythburgh. Also, similar descriptions were being reported from Dorset and elsewhere. Ipswich Record Office has the first receiving book for the Bosmere & Claydon Union House (built at Barham).

The names used in the mill scene are all taken from the 'Earl Stonham Overseers Accounts for the Poor' records for the time. Other details such as lighting of beacons, firing fields and mills with pitch and rosin are all taken from 1765 newspaper accounts. Local papers refer to embodied groups of Militia being camped close to Stowmarket. Jacob Pawsey's announcement in the newspaper is actually borrowed from a similar case in another Suffolk village.

Chapter 11

The rules for administering workhouses were published in the Ipswich Journal in August 1765. The names of paupers used here are the very ones first admitted from Earl Stonham to the Barham workhouse at its opening.

The story of the poor blind boy, George Wells, appears in the Earl Stonham Churchwarden's Accounts dated 1683.

Chapter 12

I have little evidence of what most of these boys did on leaving the school. Sam Tricker did make progress in commerce, and seeking employment with Shadrach Manning, a leading businessman of the time, seems a plausible explanation as to how he got started. Isaac Pawsey did remain in agriculture, but in time rose above his labouring roots to become a successful tenant-farmer. The Robinsons too farmed in villages round here for many years to come.

Elizabeth Warren was buried at Earl Stonham in May 1766. I do not know her cause of death or whether local surgeon, Dr. Palgrave ever attended her. Thomas Warren's marriage to Martha Palmer was at Earl Stonham the following year. There was some confusion in the register of marriage licenses. As the story shows, there also seems to have been something of a family split involving Thomas Warren and his children. His son never learned to write his own name and when he died, the schoolmaster's children would not be major recipients in his will.

Candler Bird's rhyme is taken from a contemporary newspaper.

Chapter 13

All names and statistics relating to the Bosmere & Claydon workhouse at Barham are shockingly accurate.

Chapter 14

From 1768, the Pawsey (or Parsey) family appear to have paid rent of £15 per annum on land in Earl Stonham according to Parish accounts. In 1757, Manor Court records indicate Thomas Brett having an option on land farmed previously by Thomas Garnham (his father-in-law).

Jacob Pawsey is listed as having spent just one year at the charity school. Churchwarden's accounts indicate the November 5th feast was a considerable annual parish expense.

The Tyrrells had long-owned a great deal of land in the area and were based at Gipping Hall. The Great Wood, in spite of its name, was not that large by this time and keepers had to be responsible for other assorted coverts and copses. Spring guns and man-traps were being introduced to hunting estates around this time, but more often caught land-owners and keepers themselves (see Ipswich Journals 1770-1810). Being in possession of a hempen-net at night was assumed evidence of poaching.

Chapter 15

After many years of tight financial management, the parish accounts show that Earl Stonham overspent by over £100 on building projects in 1772-3. The present day Guildhall cottages and the house in front of Halefield are described in their (Listed building) listings as being older but this may be due to the reuse of older timbers from the original Guildhall. The rental figures quoted are accurate.

Exactly how Thomas & Martha Warren made their moves remains unclear, but their final settlement in Debenham in 1776 involved their moving from Framlingham. The children's names are included in the settlement document, but the son Thomas moved back to Earl Stonham, where he trained as a wheelwright.

Chapter 16

Many details here can be verified by reference to the Earl Stonham parish registers. On the death of his father in 1764, Isaac Pawsey had been allowed to take on the tenancy of their farm at the age of just 19.

Thomas Brett married Eleanor Taylor at her home parish of Barking in March 1779. Her death in September 1881 is unexplained. Simple weddings where even the groom might merely take time off from ploughing were not uncommon (see my book, *'Lucky is the name'*.)

Chapter 17

The four Earl Stonham pubs (Cricketers, Shepherd & Dog, Angel, Brewery Tap) may or may not all have been trading at the same time. Nathaniel Studd appears in the Ipswich Journal a number of times as the licensee of the Pye (Magpie) Inn at Stonham Parva.

George Buckle was the first of the boys to marry (Mary Nunn of Battisford in 1774). They had baptised a number of children by 1781.

The name Tricker does not appear as a shop name in Stowmarket until a little later, but traders tended to keep a former owner's name if it carried goodwill with it.

PART 2

Chapter 18

It must have been confusing where so many people had the same Christian name, but there is a long tradition in Suffolk of people always being known by a nickname - see *'A short history of the village of Cotton'* by Pip Wright. The miller's daughter Debbie is one of only a few characters in the book who cannot be placed historically.

Chapter 19

Tom Brett's second wife is another shadowy character. I haven't traced a second marriage for him, but needed one for the story.

The Cherry Fair had been re-established in Stowmarket at this time. The Marriotts home at Thorney Hall has now completely disappeared.

I have no trace of James Nunn's apprenticeship, but that may be because, as described here, it was more of an informal arrangement. Mr. Tye certainly worked metals at Brockford around this time.

The deaths described are taken from local newspaper accounts and

Coroner's reports from nearby villages. Semer Hill was a known 'black spot' for carriage accidents. The Boggis family were carriers at Felsham for several generations.

James Nunn married Mary Howes at Wetheringsett in March 1793.

Chapter 20

At the Quarter Sessions in 1793, Thomas Brett was indicted to answer an accusation by Susan Subtle (or Suttle) of his being the father of her bastard child. Though I have not found further documentation, I am assuming he had to continue to pay for the child's upkeep.

Sam Tricker married Mary Pyman, the daughter of a Stowupland shopkeeper in October 1786.

Chapter 21

The cooper's business in Violet Hill appears in early trade directories, as does the Pymans' shop in Stowupland. The Stowmarket-Ipswich Navigation opened in 1793 and continued to operate successfully until the coming of the railways in the 1840s.

Chapter 22

Half of Suffolk was drinking tea bought from smugglers if you believe a fraction of the contemporary accounts. It was highly taxed and very much in demand.

Adoption of a bastard by a new father meant the 'reputed' father no longer had to pay.

In 1798, victory over the French Navy at the Battle of the Nile made Nelson even more of a national hero than he already was. The description of the town celebrations is taken from Ipswich Journal and Bury Post accounts of the time.

Smallpox continued to be a major killer disease in spite of attempts to inoculate against it. Only after vaccination became commonplace was the disease brought under control.

Chapter 23

In Winter 1800/1801, national and local papers were full of details of austerity. They also reported on footpads and highwaymen, including the story used here. Names have not been changed.

Chapter 24

Banking was one of several businesses dominated by Quaker families such as the Alexanders of Hadleigh, Ipswich and Needham Market. Tallymen were being employed to see large deliveries of malt etc. didn't go astray when sent along the navigation to Ipswich docks for export. Whit Monday Fair at Mendlesham has a long history and is a continuing tradition.

Invention of farm machinery began early with the likes of Jethro Tull, but it was unreliable and took a long time to replace man-power. As a result, later improved models were economically more sucessful.

Chapter 25

By 1900, there would be over 20 malting companies operating in Stowmarket. A century earlier, they were already beginning to expand.
The drinking houses in Stowupland Street were very much as described. The boundary then between Stowmarket and Stowupland was the River Gipping.

The National Lottery would run throughout the time of the Napoleonic wars and beyond for a number of years. Tickets were expensive and it was common to buy a fractional share such as a sixteenth.

In conclusion

Spectacles were being manufactured in 1807 by at least two 'opticians' in Ipswich, one of whom was Mr. Lyons in Carr St. (newspaper ads. and early trades directories).

Thomas Warren died two years after his wife in June 1807. He left a will - most of his worldly goods were left to John Palmer. Martha Warren's age at death was indeed given as four years older than she appears to have been.

A number of aspects of this story have been created by filling the gaps that history has left. Therefore whilst this book may not always accurately describe the genealogy of the families concerned, it has remained as true to these people and the life they lived as possible.

Thanks to...
Julia Budworth
John Jones
Roy Colchester
Trevor Brett
The staff at the Suffolk Record Offices at Ipswich & Bury St. Edmunds
British Library Newspaper Archive
Neil Langridge & Brian A. Southgate for reference to their work on Stowmarket pubs.
Several late writers of local history deserve a mention, including Harry Double, John Glyde, David Elisha Davy, & Hamlet Watling.

Alison Merry, the creator of the cover pictures.
(see www.merryilluminations.co.uk)